Also by John McManus

Born on a Train
Stop Breakin Down

Bitter Milk

John McManus

Picador　　New York

www.picadorusa.com

Picador® is a U.S. registered trademark and is used by St. Martin's Press under license from Pan Books Limited.

For information on Picador Reading Group Guides, as well as ordering, please contact the Trade Marketing department at St. Martin's Press.
Phone: 1-800-221-7945 extension 5626
Fax: 212-253-9627
E-mail: readinggroupguides@picadorusa.com

ISBN 0-312-30193-6
EAN 978-0-312-30193-4

First Edition: June 2005

10 9 8 7 6 5 4 3 2 1

For my mother, Martha Foulk McManus

Art thou the first man that was born?
or wast thou made before the hills? . . .
What knowest thou that we know not?
what understandest thou, which is not in us?

—Job 15:7-9

Bitter Milk

Chilhowee Mountain spanned Blount County at the height of twenty-six hundred feet, but Loren Garland had never in his nine years been that high. He lived with his mother at the height of a thousand feet in a long valley that remained in shadow most every morning. He had his own flower garden in the backyard, ten imaginary friends, two hundred and thirty books, and basically everything he could want. Mother didn't have a lot of extra money after her medications were paid for, but because Loren was her favorite person, she bought him all the food he needed and kept him safe from the other members of the family.

Don't let them tell you how to behave, she said. Whatever they say to do, do something else completely different, cause everything they say is useless cause they don't understand you.

The reason Mother told him so was that they didn't understand her, either. They didn't understand why she wore overalls and blue jeans and a chest binder. They didn't understand why she went by her ugly middle name of Avery rather than her beautiful first name of Opal. Avery was her mother's maiden name, but it hadn't been given to her to use. It was just decoration, and they didn't see why she was so perverse about things like that. They didn't understand why she looked androgynous or why her voice was getting deeper, or why she liked women instead of men. It didn't matter anyway, because she'd decided to be alone for the rest of her life, and for this the family didn't trust her. Loren figured he was the only one in the Black Sulphur Knobs and really the entire universe who understood Mother. This knowledge was a great burden to him.

They try to tell me I'm a bad parent, she said, because of your weight. There's nothing wrong with your weight which it's exactly fine. You don't think I'm a bad mother because of that.

Loren shook his head. Anyway I haven't seem them since I was eight, he said.

Good, she said. You don't ever need to see them again, either.

Mother didn't want Loren ever to have to feel hungry, because she was uncomfortable in her own body too, and she knew exactly how that felt. It was called gender dysphoria. Loren wasn't supposed to repeat that to anyone at his school; it was a deep secret between the two of them alone. In fact, the only one he'd ever mentioned it to was me.

You don't have dysphoria, I told him, you're just fat.

Not me; Mother. Mother does.

So she eats to make it go away?

No, Luther, it's completely different.

So when you eat, her gender diphtheria goes away.

I don't think it ever goes away.

Then why the hell does she want yours to go away?

Because I'm her son, and she's my mother.

Seems to me she'd want you to feel hungry, since misery needs company.

She's not in any misery, it's dysphoria. It's different.

That's the dumbest thing I've ever heard in my entire existence.

I talked to Loren that way only because I wanted him to stop eating so much. I thought maybe I could toughen him up, because Blount County was a backwards ignorant place where he needed to be tough. All he ever did anymore was eat. At one time we'd roamed the trails together across the hills. We'd mapped the Black Sulphur Knobs from Laws Chapel all the way to Tellico Lake, but now Loren didn't move around much; he honestly believed he had whatever he wanted.

If Mother's really got this gender misery bullshit, she doesn't love you at all, because she wants to be a man instead of a woman. When you're around, you're this constant reminder that she can never be what she wants to be.

He ate a peanut butter and blackberry jam sandwich. He ate a bowl full of potato chips, and then he poured himself a tall glass of two-percent milk.

Plus you're a boy, so there's that too. She'll probably run away from you pretty soon and never come back, especially if you keep eating so much.

Mother told me to believe the opposite of whatever you say.

You wish you were a girl, don't you.

He drank his milk and listened to Mother snore.

Does it make you sad to know you'll never be a girl?

Why would she have had me in the first place if I made her sad?

You sounded like a girl just then, when you said that. Does that make you happy?

Mother had to go to the store a lot to replace all of what Loren ate. Usually she went alone, on the same days that she had to drive all the way up to Knoxville to visit her doctor. Her insurance had finally approved the hormone shots as treatment for her ovarian cysts. If she stopped getting her period, the cysts would quit acting up as they'd done two weeks of every month for Loren's whole life. During those two weeks it was difficult to be around Mother, so Loren was always glad for the other two weeks. If you ask me, she was making the whole thing up as an excuse to be hateful and get attention. My own behavior was consistent no matter what two weeks it was, so Loren should have liked me better, but he told himself Mother was the only one he really needed. As far as he was concerned, he could spend the rest of his life alone with her. She told him not to trust kids his own age anyway. He was different than they were, and she just didn't want him to get upset when they rejected him, because that would break her heart. So they lived alone in the house, the two of them, and that was all that mattered. Mother would pick at freckles on her arm, holding them tight until blood came, and Loren would eat peanut butter and watch her digging away at her skin. They would stare out the window together from the kitchen table, looking out at Chilhowee Mountain, and that was how things went until Mamaw died, when the family had to get back together and lay eyes on each other and talk to each other and be in the same physical space. It scared Loren to sense Mother's tension. She hated to be near people, in a body like hers. She didn't like to be hugged. That was the kind of thing that made the family want to snatch Loren away from her. She told him not to worry, though. She was fine, she could handle them, they weren't going to hurt her no matter what her condition, he needed to stop worrying about her condition. If she was fixing to do anything drastic, she'd tell him.

Drastic like what? said Loren.

Like nothing. There's nothing I'll do that's drastic.

Then why did you warn me about it?

Just so you'd know nothing's wrong.

Is something wrong?

Listen, Loren, at the viewing, don't forget not to talk when they're praying. I know we don't go to church, but Ruby and Papaw and Cass and them, they like it to be quiet.

I know that, but what's wrong?

I was just trying to comfort you. You looked worried.

Loren hadn't been feeling more worried than usual, though; he always maintained that same level of worry. He couldn't help it. He worried he embarrassed Mother by being overweight. He worried about how sometimes at the grocery store in town the clerks called her *sir*. It made her mad, but if she wanted to be a man, she should have been happy about it. She didn't make sense. Sometimes Loren worried that he didn't understand her at all. He didn't understand why she wanted to go to the viewing. He knew Mother's mother had died, but it wasn't really Mamaw; it was just her dead body.

They got in the car and drove to the Primitive Baptist Church, where the viewing was held. No one's house was nice enough for a viewing, and the area was too impoverished for any funeral homes. Loren assumed the church would have no electricity or running water, but it turned out to be the Baptists who were primitive, and not the church itself. Uncle Cass was there, and Aunt Ruby, and her new husband, Dusty, and some of Mamaw's primitive friends from the church, and of course Papaw, who was probably the most primitive of all.

She should of eat more carrot, Papaw barked. Carrot makes your bowels run good.

Loren figured Papaw was sadder than the other mourners, because Papaw had known Mamaw the longest. People could do strange things when they were grieving, and Loren was dreading the actual funeral; he'd have no idea what to do. What if he jumped into the grave? He didn't know how to behave around people. There were complicated rules Mother had never taught him, because she didn't believe in them. Loren nervously observed his family from a corner of the church. Papaw belched, *Bbrrruekkchlck,* and began singing one of his songs:

I'm drunk but nobody fixed it.

Daddy, said Ruby, that one doesn't even make any sense.

That's all the words I know, he said, lighting a cigarette, and Loren held Mother's hand. She didn't like to hold hands, but this was a special time, and she didn't push him away.

You knew Mamaw the least amount of time, he said.

Least of what? she said.

Of you and Cass and Ruby, since you're youngest.

What a thing to say, Loren.

He turned red. He could never tell what was what a thing to say.

Anyway, you're wrong. You're the one knew her least. We're all older than you are.

He wanted to change the subject. How old do you think I'll be when I die? he said.

Well, Mamaw was sixty-two, and you're her grandson.

Sixty-two? Don't you want me to live longer than that?

Okay fine then, sixty-four. Sixty-five. I swan.

But it was unusual for Mother to be hateful towards Loren, because she saved her hatefulness for everybody else. He thought she was probably just grieving, so he went alone to the coffin to see Mamaw, who'd been decreased down to just ninety pounds and wasn't much to look at anymore. Loren wondered if she'd cursed him with the weight she'd lost in her last few months. In that case the fat part of him was sixty-two years old, and he shuddered, trying to think nice things about Mamaw. Would he agree to be fat forever if it would bring her back to life? He'd heard the word *deceased* wrong when he was little and had thought it was *decreased,* which made more sense, although he might have to wait until he was dead to lose any weight himself.

I dare you to reach out and touch her, I said.

Why would I want to do that?

Cause I'll be your friend if you do.

You're already my friend.

Not anymore. Now I'm your enemy.

You don't get to decide whether you're my enemy.

I'm not the one who decided it, I told him. Mother had been displeased by Loren's talks with me. She wanted to control things she had no control over. It had hurt my feelings when she'd told Loren not to talk to me anymore. It sincerely upset me, and I still haven't gotten over it. At the viewing I certainly wasn't over it. I was mad at Loren for being loyal to a crazy old boondagger like her instead of someone who really cared about him. Mother just couldn't accept the idea of authority except as something she herself possessed. She was ruining Loren's life by not admitting I was right about everything I believed. It's not arrogant of me to say so, because I don't believe that many things, so there aren't that many things I'm right about. I'm right about the things I believe, and when I questioned her authority, it was only on those things. But that was enough to make me an outlaw, and now Loren was allowed to talk to me only when we were alone. Since he talked to me far more often than that, he was disobeying Mother, which was exactly what I wanted him to do. So far, though, it hadn't gotten him anywhere.

First off, said Papaw, everone quit telling me you're sorry about Mamaw, cause I'm not one of these folks with no memory that walks in circles all night, so quit making like it wasn't them doctors. She was fine till them doctors made her die. That's how I know yuns all want me dead too. This Papaw Papaw fetch the doctor have him cut them warts from off your nose so he gets his shears and puts the warts in your blood and you've got wart blood like everbody wants you to have. Then you're dead, which I'm aware how ignart you think I am like it was some kind of ignartness in the air back in the Depression, well nothing went nowheres. That ignartness is still right here in the air. Yuns breathe it too.

Papaw had been coming closer and closer as he spoke. Now he was right in front of us.

If you think your mama's so nice and everyone else is so mean, how come she give birth to you here the middle of all this ignartness? It ain't cause I didn't bring her up right, I brought her up same as everybody else, and she was fine till you ate so much. You're just like them doctors. Stay over there with your wart blood and leave me be.

Papaw was good to have around, because he was a fool-proof indicator of when it was time to leave. Ruby and Cass and Mother and pretty much everyone agreed we'd reached that time.

It's like a sixty-pound sack of taters on your back, Papaw said as we came out the door of the Primitive Baptist Church. We were faced with a marquee: *It's not enough to love the flowers; you have to hate the weeds.* Why in tarnation would you want to haul a sixty-pound sack of taters? I'll start carrying a tater sack too and show you how ignart it looks.

Papaw was sired by pure German mountain stock that settled in these hills back before anyone around here was born. I guess it's a blessing Papaw married Mamaw, or we'd all be as tall and thin and mean and German as Papaw is. Maybe Loren could use some more tallness and thinness in him, and maybe Mother if the dysphoria thing is really her deal would want some tall-ness and meanness, but I wouldn't care for it myself. And to tell the truth Papaw's not as tall and German as he ought to be, since there's not much in the way of nutrients in the soil here, plus the whole thing with his nose. I don't have any explanation for that nose. Luckily, by the time Ruby and Cass and Mother were born, the New Deal had added some nutrients to the soil, so at least Ruby and Cass can pass for half-normal. Ruby stays pretty with all the makeup she puts on her face. She and Papaw are always getting on Loren for being so fat, but if I were Loren,

I'd point out that I don't weigh half as much as Ruby's makeup or Papaw's nose. But I'm not Loren, and the sad truth is he weighs a lot more than Ruby's makeup or Papaw's nose. Loren weighs about a hundred and fifty pounds. He probably weighs about three thousand pounds. He's not even grown yet, so who knows what he'll weigh by then. One thing he has going for him is he looks kind of smart, which doesn't get him very far here in the ignartness. These hills are called the Black Sulphur Knobs, but the valley where Papaw's land is has no name, so I might as well call it what Papaw calls it. Most of the ignartness is forested by all different sorts of trees. There are more types of trees here than in all of Europe, whatever good that does anybody.

The ones in Mother's yard were dead, and Loren was ashamed of it when Ruby and Cass and Papaw all arrived at the house for the post-viewing meal. A storm was coming, and the wind blew the dead trees into each other, causing an awful racket that was disrespectful to Mamaw's memory. One tree was already growing through the Thunderbird out in the yard. It's hard to make a tree grow through a car that fast, especially if it's dead, but Mother had managed to do it. I guess she was try-ing her best to act like a man and do yard work and keep every-thing nice. Thing is, though, Papaw had three cars growing trees and Cass had two, so Mother had a long way to go if she wanted to be a man around here.

As soon as we entered the house, she went straight to the kitchen to make food. She was determined to get the food cooked as soon as possible so the rest of the family would go home. She changed into her brick-mason shirt and put on her bandanna and limped off to the kitchen. I guess maybe one of her legs was a man's and the other was a woman's, which kept her from walking right. If that was the case, I could sympathize with her, because I like to go on long walks myself and see vari-ous vantage points of the earth. I imagine I'd be sad if I had to stop going on those long walks. Anyhow, Mother cooked in the kitchen with Ruby, which I'm sure she resented every moment of, and Cass watched fishing on the TV, and Papaw sat on the porch examining the bugs. He liked bugs the best of anything that flew. Birds and butterflies and moths and airplanes and helicopters and meteorites and angels and viruses and the cholera morbus; there wasn't anything in the world like bugs. Loren didn't like bugs as much as Papaw, and he certainly didn't like fishing, so he hovered at the doorway to the kitchen where he wouldn't be seen or heard.

Avery, that chest thing isn't gonna fool anybody.

I'm not trying to fool you.

That boy won't know whether he has a mama or a daddy.

Does it make you feel bad that you're barren, Ruby? What is it makes you want children so bad? Is it your body knows you're almost too old ever to have them, so it makes you more desperate about it every minute to try to override the decision? Not that I think it's a decision; I know how you are. I just wish I could understand, cause I don't feel that way.

You're really fixin to do it, then. All that money from the farm—

Don't stand in that doorway, Loren; go check on Papaw.

I'm sorry. I just got here. I didn't hear anything.

Go tell Papaw supper's ready and we cooked him the carrots.

He can smell it and know it's ready. I want to stay in here with you.

Don't talk to me that way, go on out to Papaw. Git!

Loren felt ashamed that she'd treat him like that in front of Ruby. Ruby might get the impression that Mother didn't like him. She'd feel sorry for him and look at him funny. She believed Loren didn't behave right as a human being, and he didn't want her to think she'd found proof. Plus he hated her name; it sounded like a kind of cat food, and I'd have to say

I agree with him. When he got to the porch, Papaw was doing his song.

Two old maids, sittin on the grass. One had her tongue in the other un's ass.

It was the only song I'd ever heard that didn't have a tune, but in this song of Papaw's there just wasn't one. Papaw had grown up with some mountain folk that didn't have much in the way of food or clothes or toothbrushes or I guess tunes.

They're serving supper, Loren told Papaw.

Two old maids, sittin in a sack. One had her fingers in the other un's crack.

Loren thought about the relationship between Mother and Papaw. Loren didn't have a father himself, and even if he had, he wouldn't be a daughter to that father, so of course he couldn't be sure, but he doubted Mother was in possession of a lot of love for Papaw.

They're serving supper, he said again.

Well they can shit, too.

Papaw, if I ask you something will you just answer it?

You wanna hear you a joke?

What's all this money everybody's talking about getting?

Why does a woman got legs?

What do you mean?

Just how come?

I don't know.

Well I be shit.

What's the matter?

I forgot what the answer is.

It's probably the same reason men do.

No it's not, peckerhead, it's a joke. It's no reason for it at all.

When Loren went back into the house, Ruby had set out beef stew, corn, okra, fried potatoes, biscuits, dumplings, minute steak, lemonade, gravy, dressing, beets, yellow squash, some other squash, and of course some carrots so our bowels could run good. Loren scooted two of the place mats apart and put a sixth chair at the table and went for silverware.

Oh, sweetie, Ruby said. Did you forget Mamaw's passed?

No, said Loren, I haven't forgotten.

What are you doing with the table, then? There's five of us.

I'm setting another place, just in case.

We don't need another place. I'm the one doin it.

Now if I had been Loren, which thank God I'm not, I'd have said, How the hell do you know what I need and don't need, you old cat-food-looking hag?

What if someone drops their plate? asked Loren.

Then they'll clean it up and go get a new plate. Law law.

Will yuns shut up so I can hear the fishing? yelled Cass.

Loren was getting frustrated, so he recited the alphabet backwards in his mind to calm himself down. Ruby didn't know how to talk to him, and sometimes she could work things up into an awful fright, but eventually Mother always came to the rescue.

Just let him set the table how he wants, she called from the kitchen.

Loren's heartbeat calmed. Maybe Mother wasn't sad from the viewing anymore and she'd act normal again, he thought.

Well I'm off to the turkey shoot, said Cass, rising from the couch.

Cass, said Ruby, your own blood mother is just passed.

This is the most important one of the entire season.

So it's even more important than the other turkey shoots.

Either that's a dumb joke or you're just plain dumb.

Cass got his leather jacket and left. We could hear Papaw singing more of his tuneless Two Old Maids song; then the door slammed, so that the singing faded.

Now we'll have entirely too much to eat, said Ruby. Every

time someone dies, it goes just like this. Why I'll bet you wish you could go to that turkey shoot too, don't you, Avery? This is just an awful disaster. Loren, you're so lucky to be an only child. You people and your turkeys and your fish and I don't suppose I'll ever see the end of it.

Mother was ignoring Ruby. She went over to Loren and said, You don't need to set another place after all. Luther can sit at Cass's place.

Oh so *that's* it, Ruby said. Really Lorn why does it even need a chair?

Loren's heartbeat started doing its thing again. It's not an it, he said, it's a him.

Why does it need a plate? So you can eat more yourself?

I'm not even hungry, said Loren, which was of course bull-shit.

I suppose you'll eat your little friend's plate up too. Well I swan.

Mamaw had always said *swan*, but it was hick talk, so Ruby usually just swore instead.

She turned red. I'm not just saying these things just to say it, she cried.

Then why are you saying them in the first place? said Mother.

It might as well be little kittens. They're real. They piss and shit.

I'll piss your damn shit, Papaw called from the porch.

I liked Papaw best of all. He made more sense, because he told people why they said the things they said. Plus he never came inside to eat. When we started eating, I sang his song at the top of my lungs so Loren couldn't even enjoy his food. Loren's the kind of person who it takes a lot to make him not enjoy food. Papaw's refusal to eat with us did nothing to hinder Loren's enjoyment of his food. I myself couldn't even hinder any-thing related to his food. You'd think I could do whatever I wanted to him, but it's a complicated relationship between Loren and me, and he likes to think he controls it by believing or not believing I exist. Actually I control it by believing or not believing that he himself exists. Since Loren always exists, I always believe it; I'm therefore always in control, though controlling the relationship doesn't mean I control Loren.

Lorn, said Ruby, there's gonna be more money, now that Mamaw's passed.

Why wouldn't Papaw get all her money?

Sometimes things is more complicated, kind of complexlike.

Loren, said Mother, why don't you take your Papaw some food.

Why are you being this way all the time?

What way? The way that wants your Papaw to eat food?

He told me he doesn't want any food.

Loren, don't lie to me on a day like this, now take him some food.

Somehow Mother always knew it as soon as he wasn't telling the truth. Also she was treating Loren like he was a child. He thought they had an agreement: she'd treat him the way he wanted to be treated, and he'd treat her the way she wanted to be treated, too.

Papaw likes okra, Ruby said. Give him lots of okra, it makes your legs long.

Okra tastes like mangy dog balls, I said.

He'll come in and eat when he's finished singing, said Loren.

So you can't stop your own eating long enough to take your Papaw a plate?

Ruby reached across and scooped some okra onto my plate. The food around here has some real special powers: the broccoli puts hair on your chest, the tomatoes keep your piss clear, and the okra cleans the rot out of your gut. It's got nothing to do with how long your legs are; it's your gut. I figure someday we'll be rich from all these special-powered vegetables. Loren filled my plate up with them and went out. On the porch Papaw took it and pointed to where the first stars shone and said, See where they ain't no stars.

Loren looked up to only five stars visible in the sky.

That's the moon, said Papaw.

It's a new moon tonight.

Tell me it ain't there.

It's not there.

The hell it's not there.

You told me to tell it to you.

Well I've been around. I know about things.

The moths swarming around the porch light carried awful diseases, I had told him. If you got bit the doctors cut your arm off. Loren trusted what I said was true because I was born first. Like Papaw, I had been around and I knew about some things.

Two old maids, sittin in a truck, sang Papaw, and then he stopped and said, You know what the rest of that joke is?

I want you to answer the question I asked you.

Don't you get it how a joke works? I ast you a question about why something is, then you say no why, then I say why, and that last why there, that's the joke.

Then why do women have legs?

Anyhow I'll answer your durn question. Cause we've got to sell the land to pay for all your food. Now that your Mamaw's passed we can get shet of it once and for all. Anyhow it was sold anyways, but it's a good thing for the money then, you think your mama wants to stay here in all this ignartness? Your mama likes to live up high above other people cause she thinks she's better than everone. I might build a even higher place to show her who's who. That'd show her who's who. It quits there at the top of that hill, though, cause if I owned the whole Chilhowee Mountain I'd get rid of all those trees and write some words up there. I might just put my songs up there. It don't take nothing to write a song, you just write one line and then another line. That one's got to rhyme with the first line. That's how you know what to say. I don't know who owns that mountain, but whoever it is don't have much to say. Probably it's them Indian folk who they've been breathing the air here longern any of us is how come they don't know what to do with a piece of land. Figger my songs might do folks some mighty good. Even them Indians could sing it cept that they have a different alphabet and can't read. If they wanted my songs up there in their alphabet, they had hundreds of years to do it in, and that mountain don't say a blame thing. Thanks to that mountain, won't none of us ever see a sunrise. Time the sun's rose, it's done afternoon, for our whole lives. Course it's a different story on the other side. I wonder what it says over there on that other side. Probly a bunch of Indian talk. Those Indians, they like the sun. I reckon they're over there right now on that other side of the mountain without their clothes on, writhing around in the sun like cats in catnip, getting red.

Eventually Mother and Ruby joined us outside to watch the lightning approach.

Lightning's comin, Mother said.

That dead hickory's gonna go.

Not before those two dead poplars.

But I ain't gone over there none, said Papaw.

That chestnut there with its chestnut blight, said Ruby.

No, I've pretty much stayed right here.

Is that what those disease spot things are? said Mother.

I ain't one to haul potaters up and down the mountain, said Papaw.

No that's the maple, said Ruby, that's maple blight or some like.

Are you already finished eating? asked Loren.

Already? said Papaw. You been in there for forever. Maybe we ort to get you a mule to haul around you and your potaters. Course I guess you pretty much keep your taters planted right here on this porch. Shame a tater don't do nothing for you, way a carrot does.

It began to rain. Rain, said Mother. Ruins the whole damn day.

Loren wanted to say something, so that people would look at him and see how fat he was—I can't think of any other reason for him to talk—but there wasn't anything to say. I guess that's why he asked where butterflies went when it rained.

I don't guess they go anywhere except where they already are.

But it kills them just to touch their wings.

Well I guess a tater puts hair on your chest, said Papaw.

Maybe they go into the birdhouses or the mountain caves, said Mother.

Ruby clenched her eyes shut. Oh, Avery. You don't make sense.

It felt strange to Loren to hear his mother called by her name instead of just Mother. He supposed she looked enough like an Avery, but the name Avery was a matter of some conflict, and Loren didn't like conflict. Even his own name had some conflict. It was a boy's name, but people always thought it was a girl's, and no one liked it when he acted like a girl. They assumed his name was the culprit. He suspected they wanted to replace it with a more manly name, but he liked it the way it was. For one thing, it sounded pretty; for another, the way everyone pronounced it reminded him of the word *forlorn*. He liked his last name, too. Garland was what Christmas trees were decorated with. Loren Garland was a fitting name for him, and he was thankful for it.

You reckon we'll get hit by lightning this time? said Ruby.

No, said Mother, I'd say it'll pass over like it does most other times.

Loren liked electric storms. He could feel in the air how people were listening, bracing for the future. It was relaxing. He liked for Mother and Ruby to talk to each other. Mother acted happy, talking to her sister. If she seemed like she was happy for a long enough time, maybe she'd realize she actually was happy. He wanted the best for her. She allowed him to worry about her incessantly, which if you ask me was negligence, and I planned to get him away from her as soon as possible.

Course that's the last thing you need, Avery, is hair on your chest.

Mother decided to kick Papaw out of her house. Loren hadn't seen anything like it for a long time. She stood up and began to scream. Half her voice was woman, half was man. This was the first time she'd been around her father in almost a year, and she'd been saving it up about how she wanted him out of her sight never to come back. I paid close attention, because it was exciting and interesting. Papaw, on the other hand, didn't pay much attention at all. He sang his Two Old Maids song some more. They sat in a sack. Then they sat in a lunt. I could hardly hear the song over Mother's yelling, especially since it still had no tune, but Mother somehow managed to hear it.

There's no such thing as a lunt, she said.

You'd know if you wasn't so busy sittin on it.

But she wasn't sitting; she was standing and waving her arms because she was fed up with his inability to make sense, although that was what I liked about him. Sometimes people make the most sense when they don't make any sense at all, if that makes sense.

I sure wish it was your twin that'd lived, said Papaw, and not you.

Last time it was Ruby had the twin, Mother said.

Well then this time it's you.

If you're gonna lie, at least remember what you lie.

Maybe it's the twin that was a girl, and you smothered it up inside of her.

Then is those two old maids spose to be twins too? said Ruby.

Well, it was a long time ago, anyway.

Mother forced them to leave, although whether or not they'd obey her command never to show their faces again was a question for another time. Loren was astonished at how long a day it had been. Nothing else important could possibly happen for quite a while, except finishing his food, which wasn't even there, because Ruby had thrown it all away. Mother screeched away down the driveway in her Chevette, leaving Loren alone to eat the white part out of all the Oreos. That made him tired, and he decided to go to bed. He always wore his regular clothes to bed. The bedroom door wouldn't lock, so he tried to change clothes as little as possible, in case someone saw him changing. That was fine with Mother if he didn't want to change, because times were hard and there wasn't much money for bedclothes.

Loren got in bed, put his hands together, and whispered, God bless Mother and Papaw and Mamaw and Ruby and Cass and everyone who doesn't have as much as me.

Pretty soon, he thought, he'd have to take Mamaw's name out, since she was dead and all. He thought he'd wait at least one week before taking her out.

How come you don't pray my name? I said.

He jerked his hands apart so I wouldn't see him praying. I did pray your name, he said, you just didn't hear it.

Am I one of those people who doesn't have as much as you?

I meant poor people, like starving children.

I don't have as much fat as you, so maybe so.

You can pray your own name, Luther.

Then God bless my own name.

He pulled the covers over his head, but his pulse was a hundred and thirty, far too fast to sleep. He measured his pulse about four hundred times a day, just in case. Most of the times were at night, when his mind would keep him awake for hour after hour.

Get dressed, I said, let's go out to the woods. The red bud trees are blooming.

Since when do you care about blooming trees?

Just do it. This is one of those times when you just do what I say.

As I've explained, it's a complicated relationship between me and Loren. It would be nice if he had multiple personalities, in which case I could pretend to be one of his other personalities and he'd have to do what I say, but he's quite sane, and I doubt Mother or anyone else would believe it. And one of us would have to be the dominant personality, which isn't what I want. I'm not trying to control anyone. All I want is for people to be happy. In this particular valley, between these particular mountains, Loren has the best chance of it. If he'd just start thinking of me as someone here to help, everything would fall into place—but he lay there thinking it was unhealthy to be out late at night, people died of that kind of thing, in books at least, and Loren wasn't taking any risks. He snuck into the kitchen for a midnight snack and opened the refrigerator. It would have been a great thing, the two of us, the mountains all around, the clouds trailing through the night sky. He opened the onion dip and set it on the table. Mother was home again, and she was snoring. Outside, the thunder was as low as her snores. We would have dodged between the hailstones. But I wasn't trying to be mean, taunting him with these thoughts. I just wanted someone to play with.

Loren pinched a bag of chips apart and dipped them into the

lode of white cream. Wouldn't it last a long time! He scraped only the edges so it wouldn't look like he'd eaten as much as he had. Chives fell like confetti onto the surface film of the spread. He scooped them up with more chips so as not to leave a trace. He didn't feel full anymore.

Better say your prayers again, I said. If you eat after you pray, the prayer won't count. You'll just shit the words back out with the chips.

Words aren't real, you can't touch them.

Why would you go and touch your shit?

You're not making any sense.

They'll fall in the septic tank with the rats. Rats will answer your prayers instead of God.

Loren wished they could pay a doctor to help him stop eating. His stomach felt extremely bad now. Miss Rathbone, his teacher for the fourth grade, had said the word *bad* was overused. He could say wretched or putrid or horrid, instead. He knew it would get rid of five or six hundred calories to throw up, but he wasn't big on trying new things. There were plenty of old things, and he just stuck with those, mostly. Maybe it wouldn't get light in the morning; school wouldn't happen if everybody just stayed asleep, all through the Black Sulphur Knobs.

If you stay home from school tomorrow, I said, I'll never speak to you again.

Why do you want me to be at school if I feel so horrid?

Mother doesn't want you here at the house all day.

But my stomach hurts and my ears hurt and my throat hurts and my hair hurts and I can't breathe right.

What makes you think Mother likes to spend so much time with you? Don't you think she'd homeschool you if she wanted to be with you all day like that?

She wants to homeschool me, but she doesn't know enough, or she would.

So Miss Rathbone knows more than Mother.

I guess so. I don't know.

I'm gonna steal her paddle from her tomorrow.

Why would you do that?

So she'll paddle me, dumbass.

There was a complicated thing going on with paddling and staying home from school. Eli, who was Dusty's son and Loren's stepcousin, had been paddled thirty-four times, the exact number of days Loren had stayed home from school. Loren hadn't really been sick, but Eli hadn't really done anything wrong, either. It was a contest to see who could get the higher number, but no one except Loren knew about it, and if they did, they'd root for Eli, because getting paddled was a more admirable thing than staying home sick. But Loren couldn't imagine doing anything against the rules, so I had decided to have a paddling contest with Eli to help Loren get comfortable with the idea of doing things wrong and breaking rules. Maybe next year in the fifth grade Loren could participate in a paddling contest himself. Making wagers was fun, and I tried to get Loren into the spirit by making one with him: if I won against Eli, Loren had to do it next year. This bet was the reason I threatened Loren not to stay home from school. How was I supposed to get paddled if we weren't even there? I was fed up with how much he dreaded school. It tore up his stomach to dread things so much; in fact he probably had very little chance of living to adulthood, so he figured he might as well get paddled now, so the other kids would like him, while he was still alive, so he tried preparing himself for it, which scared him, reminding him of school in general, thus causing him dread that made him sick so he could stay home one more day.

How can she paddle you if you steal her paddle?

She'll get that one from the principal with the holes in it.

Where are you going to hide it?

Nowhere if you stay home and stuff your face all day.

That's not true about Mother.

Go ask her, then.

She's sleeping.

Wake her up. I bet she's dying to spend more time with you.

Loren didn't obey me right away. He fell asleep and had a dream in which Mother was rooted to the ground like a tree. She turned brown from the bark and sprouted flowers made of sparkleberry pulp and ate her own corollas. Loren was all in a mess over it when he woke up, so he went to make sure she wasn't rooted to the carpet or anything.

That's a terrible nightmare, said Mother. You don't have to worry about me doing a thing like that. I hate trees. They just stay in one place forever. It takes them years and years to rot.

That one that fell on the garage is rotting.

Years and years and years and years and years.

Is there medicine to stop having nightmares? What if I wake up and I'm dead?

You couldn't, you'd be dead. Better just try to get back to sleep.

Loren didn't know what smelled so sharp and rainy in the air. He didn't have a word for what was brooding in his stomach; he couldn't remember certain faces. Fireflies breathed the darkness out of sumac as he lay awake determining whether or not I was right, whether Mother was miserable to have brought him into the world. If she was, he thought, she tried her best to carry on, speaking to him sometimes, making new things for him, answering certain questions and leaving others unanswered, spending most of her time out of sight, hibernating until the dread soured in his stomach, when she would embark on her next stage of life without him. But it had been too long a day for anything else to happen. He blamed me for putting the idea in his head at all. Better to believe she loved him and wanted

him to exist. For one thing, she'd said so; for another, it seemed
to upset her when he was sick, and that was why he tried so hard
to will himself to go to school. When he woke up, he thought,
he'd get on the bus and go to school. The alarm would sound at
6:30, and he'd go out and wait for the bus to school. He'd get
dressed and have breakfast and it would be time to begin
school. This was the one thing Mother and I agreed on wanting
him to do, but it was her worry, not my threats, that caused him
to do it. After lying awake for five hours and sleeping three, he
did it. He got ready, ate a bowl of cereal with milk and then two
spoonfuls of peanut butter, got on the bus, and sat there dreading school, watching morning fog swirl around the top of Chilhowee Mountain while I planned where I'd hide the paddle:
below ground, beneath the foundation of the schoolhouse, under the playground where worms would eat it and taste of my
dead skin, which they liked, I explained to Loren. Then, as
Loren had feared it would do, the bus pulled into the parking lot
of the school.

Yuns had better just sit there and shut up.

Miss Rathbone had favorite words that she liked better than
any others, like *horrendous*. I'm in a horrendous mood, she told
us. Yuns had better just sit there and shut up, the whole day.

The portable classroom was painted nicotine-yellow to match
Miss Rathbone's hair, and there was a special kind of clock that
moved exactly as slowly as the earth did around the sun. Shut
up! she'd hiss every few minutes. Loren was scratching his scabs
off as she explained fractions. He had caused scabs to form by
picking at his arms like Mother did, and now he picked at the
scabs until one began to bleed. Miss Rathbone lifted a piece of
jumbo chalk, which was the only kind she could write with because she was so blind, and it fell in two.

Who did that? she demanded. Which one of you tore my
chalk up?

I did, Eli said. You wanna paddle me for it?

I had been careless, and now Eli would win. I made sure to seem upset about this development. I wanted Loren to understand there were other people in the world I was involved with, like Eli, and he wasn't the only one. Loren was interested in Eli, too. He couldn't take his eyes off Eli's face sometimes. It was only that he wanted to look like Eli, he thought. That was the only way to explain it, because it was girls he wanted to be friends with, not boys. The girls in his class didn't understand they'd enjoy playing with him. They couldn't see that he was really much more of a girl than a boy. There were girl things on the playground that only girls could do, and Loren tried not to be sad about it when they would run away from him.

Write this down, Miss Rathbone was shouting, but Loren was busy holding his scab shut so it wouldn't bleed on his new shirt from Sears.

I don't care how good your memory is, write it down! I've had it up to here with your smarty-pants crap. How can I learn you fractions when you treat me like this?

Miss Rathbone tried to smack Loren upside the head, but he moved his arm to block hers, so she ended up only smacking him upside the arm, which got his blood on her. When she waved her hand to try to shake the blood off, Eli jumped up.

Sit your little butt down in that chair, she yelled.

You was gonna get that blood on me. That's how you get AIDS.

Rudolph and Lyhugh and Leland and the other Leland all laughed.

You best hush your mouth, Miss Rathbone warned.

Okay, just don't touch me no more.

One more word, I'll call the principal over the intercom.

Don't rub your face like that. Now you've got AIDS on your face.

Loren wouldn't have thought somebody's chest bones could

curl around themselves, but that was what hers did when she got her paddle out to give Eli number thirty-five. Get up to the desk and bend over, she ordered, you know how it works. She paddled and paddled him as Loren dabbed at blood with a page of his science book. Eli got fifteen licks, three times the usual number, so it counted as numbers thirty-five, thirty-six, and thirty-seven. Now I'd never catch him.

Loren couldn't deny his jealousy of Eli and of the camaraderie Eli had formed with the rest of the class after only two months of living here in the ignartness. Eli had moved to the ignartness from Knoxville, where Dusty had learned all his developer knowledge. Maybe I was jealous of Eli too, Loren thought, so I berated him for comparing himself to me that way. I was exactly who I wanted to be, I told him; could he say that of himself?

Does it make you mad when I laugh at you? asked Eli when Miss Rathbone was finished. Cause I think it would make me mad, if I was you.

Loren got nervous when people weren't nice to each other. It made Miss Rathbone nervous too, I guess, because she called the principal over the intercom. Mr. Ownby came to the classroom and flicked the lights, which meant to listen, and he said, Listen. When we listened, he only whispered to Miss Rathbone, who for some reason got to go home for the rest of the day. She ought to have been grateful, though of course she wasn't, and neither was Mr. Ownby; he was disappointed with us, and angry. Mr. Ownby was a strange little excuse for a man. He looked like he might blow away from the force of Miss Rathbone's breath as she huffed out the door. We were all responsible, said Mr. Ownby, so we spent the rest of the day copying down the dictionary. Mr. Ownby wasn't scary and old and twisted and arthritic like Miss Rathbone. Except for the fact he wasn't fat, he looked enough like Loren to be his father, but Loren was too dumb to wonder about stuff like that. Mother didn't like men, and Loren never considered how he might have come about. To picture Mother with a man made him cringe and tighten up and feel sorry for her. He wanted to protect her from the outside world, and Mr. Ownby was the outside world. He refused to look at Mr. Ownby as he copied the dictionary with his right hand and held the page from his science book to his arm with his left. Bleeding without a cut meant cancer, and although he'd picked the scab open himself, he didn't remember where the scab had come from in the first place, unless it was another scab he'd picked, in which case the origins of that older scab were themselves suspect. He didn't want to die of cancer. That wouldn't be right for him. Radon caused cancer; teflon on skillets caused cancer. It got inside food and burned holes in people's bodies, and he'd been meaning to throw Mother's teflon skillets away, and he kept them in mind as he wrote, and all the way home on the bus. When he got home, he took them and hid them in the crawlspace beneath the house while Mother slept in the rocker. She looked so uncomfortable, as though her body was pushing her out. She slept more than twelve hours a day now. It was incredible to watch the time grow.

Let's go out to the woods, I said.

I'm supposed to remind Mother to take her medicine.

She'll be mad at you if you wake her up.

Mother doesn't get mad at me.

Why do you think she's asleep in the first place?

Because her mother just died?

Would you sleep all the time if Mother died?

Don't talk about if Mother died.

What about me? What if I died?

How could you die? That's impossible.

If you decided you wanted me to die, I guess I'd die.

I don't want anybody to die.

You don't want to be fat, either, but you are.

To tell the truth, I wasn't sure I wanted to keep existing at all. No one had ever given me that choice. That was one thing Loren could do that I couldn't. It would have been so easy, in a place like this, with all those farming implements in the shed, and if I'd had a body too, I'd have done it. Of course, there are aspects I'd enjoy in a body: lachrymal ducts, with which to weep, so I could see how that feels, or pheromones, to cause people to want to be near me. Loren didn't have those either. If he'd tapped into these thoughts of mine and thought them too, we might have bonded over it and grown closer, but he only sat picking foam from the couch cushion. At night we had a staircase into each other's dreams, and I wanted us together, walking the trails at night, but Mother had spoken of murderers who came out past sunset, roaming across the galax and the sphagnum moss to kill him dead. He tried to stay away from the bag of pecans; he took only a handful to dip into the ice cream. The day had gone well—he'd eaten so little—but the pecans were thick and smoky and he filled himself full of them. There was a jar of cashews in the cabinet. He hoped Mother would find him eating them and lock him in a foodless room until he was thin.

Mother finally woke up and came straight to the kitchen for nuts.

Where's the pecans? There was a whole jar.

There's some cashews left. Did you sleep well?

She sighed and went to her room and came out with her shoes on.

Are you going to the grocery store? he asked.

I want to be alone awhile.

But you were asleep for three hours. Can I come with you?

So now I only get to be alone while I sleep?

Will you get some more peanut butter at the store?

We just got some, Loren. I don't think you should have more peanut butter.

I ate it gradually. It's only for sandwiches, Mother, I promise.

She told him she would, kissed him good-bye, and went out the door. We listened to the sound of the engine fading away. Then I told Loren one more time how I cared more for him than Mother did, because she was the one who bought him food. I'd been saying it over and over since the beginning of it all, and I don't like to repeat myself, but folks around here have a way of not listening to things. They're the best nonlisteners of anyone in the world. If anyone ever comes to discover this ignartness, the ability not to listen may make us as rich as the vegetables surely will.

Things were changing, though, or had been changing, so I made plans for what to say to Mother when she got home. I'd been planning this for a long while, and I was only making my final touches. Loren of course didn't notice, because he was in the kitchen watching the clock. He didn't like to be in the kitchen, because it caused him to eat, but he had to make sure Mother wasn't taking too long. She was always out driving, trusting her life to strangers. Men drove drunk; Loren had heard them bragging that it was more fun that way. There were teenagers who played chicken at Suicide Bend. Would Mother swerve in time?

I was worried about you, Loren said to her when she got home.

What were you worried about? What for? Help me carry these in.

She had bought Chips Ahoy cookies, Soft Batch cookies, cheddar cheese, American cheese, buttermilk, a bag of Ruffles, and of course pecans, but no peanut butter. There weren't any special-powered vegetables. Mother was trying to prove her bowels could run good and her gut could stay free of gripe and hair could even grow on her chest no matter what kind of food she ate.

You hungry, Loren? I'll make some grilled cheese. Get me a skillet.

He pretended not to have heard her.

I said get me a skillet. What's the matter with you? Aren't you hungry?

She buttered both sides of a slice of bread, and Loren bent down and rummaged through the cabinet as if looking for skillets, knocking pans and trays together.

I don't see the skillets anywhere.

Loren, don't be dumb, just find them.

I'm not very hungry. I only want one sandwich.

I have to eat too, what about my sandwich?

There's the cookies and cheese and chips you bought, and pecans.

Those are the desserts. They're for after our real food. I swan, what in heaven's name have you done with my skillets? I try to feed you and you try to stop me. Go to your room.

Sending Loren to his room was the only thing she ever did to punish him, since he'd always cried too much if she spanked him. Anyway, they were friends on equal footing with each other, so it wasn't a punishment at all; it was just a way of being alone. He shut the kitchen door and paced up and down the hallway. I paced up and down the hallway with him, but he was still mad at me for saying that I loved him more than Mother did, so he wasn't paying attention. I was sick of this. It was time to go into action. I reentered the kitchen without him. Mother was slurping her grape juice from a plastic wineglass. The angels stood watch beneath their golden halos on the wallpaper. The gates of heaven rose beside them from a bowl of fruit. She was looking into the mirror above the sink as she washed dishes and ran dishwatery fingers through her hair.

Where do you even come from? she said into the mirror.

I was tired of walking up and down in the hallway, I said.

And have you considered Loren? What will you do about Loren?

He always lies to you, I said, but you believe him.

Mother frowned to herself and said, Why are you even here?

I've never lied to you once, and you hate my guts.

Mother felt her Adam's apple and made it move up and down her throat. She seemed saddened by it. She moved over to the stove and placed a saucepan on the stove eye and cut slices of cheddar cheese.

He'll still love me no matter what happens, she whispered. Why am I even worried about it?

You want to bet on it? I said. You want to make a little wager?

Mother put the sandwich in the saucepan to fry and moved back to the mirror. Soapsuds dribbled from her hair as she spoke to the glass.

You can do whatever you want, she said. Who gives a shit what the consequences are? Do whatever you want. I don't care what happens. This is your life, too.

She nodded and said no more. As far as I could tell, this meant she'd turned Loren over to me to teach him what I wanted once and for all.

I'm fixing you your sandwich, she called out.

Is that all you two can talk about to each other? I said.

You'd do good to let me, she said.

Well, this'll stop you from turning him against me any more.

Why are you so mean to me? she murmured, and in the hall Loren wondered if she hated him. Maybe she'd leave because of the skillets he'd hidden. He was sorry they were gone. What if Mother killed herself over it? He prayed for her to go to bed so he could eat more Chips Ahoy cookies. He cracked the door to get a glimpse of her. She was leaning against the oven looking old, fanning herself with a *Better Homes and Gardens*. She was always too warm, because she wore several layers of shirts to hide the shape of her body. There was a hole in her jeans, and Loren could see she still hadn't shaved her legs. He couldn't remember the last time he'd seen her smile. He shut the door again and pressed his cheek against the living room wall until it hurt. He wished it were for her sake that he wanted to be thin, so she could be proud of him.

Okay, she said to herself, let's give this a shot.

So I followed Loren onto the front porch where we stood together in the shadow of the mountain, watching the sky grow dim. The forsythias he'd planted along the front of the house for their pretty yellow flowers weren't blooming. In fact they had no buds at all. He went to them and felt a twig. It snapped off. It seemed they'd perished from the late frost. The hibiscus had died too a while back. And of course the pyracanthas were dead. Ruby liked to say important things when people died, how they lived on in us, but Loren hoped these bushes wouldn't live on in him; he didn't want to get any bigger. He went back to the porch and sat on a cedar plank and despaired. He dug the dirt crescents from beneath his toenails to shave weight from his total, because even his other imaginary friends had started making fun of him for being fat. They hadn't gotten to spend much time with him in quite a while, because I was so powerful now. I decided it was time for them to die. There were ten who died, three girls and seven boys. Joanna drowned, and Shane succumbed to fever. Gus and Rachel cleaved themselves with swords. Spit and Ike and Justin burned up in a fire, and their ashes were carried away in the storm that swallowed Caleb, Seth, and Sonny up its funnel, spun them round the earth and pulverized their bodies on the scarp of Chilhowee Mountain. Loren buried them all in a row by the old sandbox and marked their graves with arrowheads and didn't ask why I alone had escaped to tell the story.

So many things were dying in Loren's mind, ideas mostly, the thought that all was as it should be, the confidence that things wouldn't end. Still, he loved Mother and he ate the grilled cheese she'd made him, along with a sweet gherkin and a handful of salted and peppered potato chips, and afterwards she asked him if he wanted to go on a drive. He was suspicious, because she never wanted to go anywhere anymore. It had to do with the state of her mind. It upset her to see how other people were living when she had to live as she lived. So he tried not to say yes too vigorously. Maybe he'd get to go all the way to another state. He'd never been to one before. The sun was just beginning to set when he ducked his head under the fallen cherry tree to get in the Chevette. Mother, already in the driver's seat, turned the ignition and flooded the engine with gas. She prided herself on what a good driver she was, and Loren loved riding with her. Gravel shot up every which way as we backed down the driveway. We drove north on Stump Road, and then we went west and north and east and up and down on various other roads; that's how the roads are around here, spread across the land as if someone had spilled a can of worms. Mother pointed out butterfly weed in a ditch on Chota Road among the wild carrots. I was watching her carefully to make sure she wouldn't cheat and violate the terms of our wager, but she seemed to be holding up her end of the deal. She said a whole bunch of flower names like toadshade, fleabane, purslane. She was one of those special people who knows the name of every flower and tree and bird and fish. It's hard to say whether she really knew them or was just making them up. We passed the Primitive Baptist Church, where Mamaw's hole had already been dug for the funeral the next morning. Then Mother pulled into a gravel driveway. We couldn't see a house, but the mailbox said *Carnetta Sledge,* and Mother let the car idle awhile and then turned it off.

Mother, we shouldn't be here. We don't know who lives here. Mother, we're sitting in someone's *driveway.*

Do you remember what I told you about?

She turned to him and seemed to laugh, but the noise ended as soon as it had begun. Loren saw how sad her eyes looked. She wasn't supposed to have gray hairs at thirty-five.

About what? He said it louder: What?

The flowers, she said eventually.

What about the flowers?

Is it ironweed or butterfly weed that's purple?

I think it's ironweed.

You sound like you don't know.

I don't need to know, because you know.

You hear the words and you don't see any colors.

I think it's ironweed, Loren said.

I don't remember, either. I don't have any idea.

Soon, I thought, the man who owned this driveway would appear with a shotgun. He'd kill Mother first so Loren would have to watch her die. Loren wanted to die first himself, but then Mother would see it, and she'd suffer. He was a man and she was a woman, so he should be the one to suffer if there was suffering, but he didn't want to.

I'm sorry I wasn't listening better, he said.

It was my fault, not yours.

I'll ask Miss Rathbone.

That woman's as ignart as anybody. Don't go bothering her.

If Mother were still in school, Loren thought, she'd be in the thirty-second grade.

Can we get out of this driveway now? he said.

What is it you're in such a hurry for?

He couldn't think of what to say to make Mother understand. He shouldn't have to explain it; mothers were the ones who were supposed to explain things. They were supposed to make their children feel safe.

I was gonna tell you something, but I can't if you're staring like you want something.

You'd better watch out, I warned her. Don't give it away. That'll ruin it.

There's nothing I want, said Loren. Go ahead and tell me what you were going to tell me.

You just said there's nothing you want, Loren.

I want to know what you were telling me.

Whatever it is, I warned, you better not tell him.

Whose driveway is this? he said.

You don't know her. It's just some driveway.

I had nothing to worry about, I knew then, because whatever she wanted to tell him, she was too ashamed. Maybe it was her wager with me, or maybe it was something else. I'm not ashamed of the wager, but I accept myself for what I am. What I am is what I am, and I see no reason to make people think I'm anything other than that.

Loren felt calmer when Mother put the car in reverse. Out on the road no one could shoot us; roads belonged to everyone. The trumpet flowers in dark gullies never made a sound. Just before home, I saw where our old fort in the woods had been. The squirrels had been the soldiers; we'd been the Cherokee. The leaves were bastard swords. Loren had clutched a brittle stem and stabbed himself and fallen into my arms. His sword was brown and crumbled to the earth; it was October, in the time of dying leaves, when he'd still been thin enough to take his shirt off. I saw that the leaves had rotted into dirt, covering the rocks and logs we'd gathered, so the fort could no longer be said to exist. All Loren wanted to know now was why Mother was mad at him. There were several reasons why she might have hurried to bed without goodnight or even putting away the butter and cheese; she might have been upset about Mamaw, she might have been unhappy in general, her troubles might have been acting up. They got worse each time, and Loren wished he could feel it in his own body for a while, so the two of them could understand each other.

Think about yourself more, I said. It's too late for her. Let's get out of here.

I can't get out of anywhere, I'm nine years old.

There are places where things happen.

Things happen here, too.

Like watching the mirror to keep from eating?

We share a first memory: I was in the crawlspace. I'd asked Mother why I should ever listen to what she said, and she had banished me. She was fixing red velvet cake; it was our birthday. Loren stood above me, in the house, ignoring what I told him through the floor. He watched Mother stir the ingredients together. Mother spread icing onto the cake and looked upon her work and nodded. I had to stay in the crawlspace for fifteen minutes. Maybe it was longer. I walked up and down its bald dirt slope. I grew to love that space and hid in its dark mold many a time.

Loren ate some peanut butter crackers, some apple butter crackers, and a bowl of applesauce. He watched the road through the living room window, and though he knew it wasn't an important road he imagined it full of travelers bound for faraway places. A thin crescent moon rose above Chilhowee Mountain. Whenever Loren looked at the moon, he stopped being bored for a moment. He wished there were a hundred things like looking at the moon to do each day, so the days would be a hundred moments shorter. He walked along the border of the yard where we'd played freeze tag a long time ago. When we were eight, a year was an eighth of our lives; now we were nine, and it was a ninth, which meant our lives were getting shorter. Mother said every year was twice as short as the last, which meant we'd be half dead at eleven, and Mother was already four-fifths dead. Her body was dying around her mind. That was why she wanted out of it.

He decided to stay awake until sunrise and see if all those hours were really there. Eventually he was in a deep nightmare that I caused by moving myself into his blood. This wasn't easy, and before long he dreamt a heart attack. You best not die, I said in the dream, they'll have to buy your coffin in the husky section. Things are more expensive in the husky section. Mother needs every last penny of this money she's getting. We made a bet. As soon as she gets that money, she's out of here.

When his heart attack had finished killing him, he awoke. Mother was bent over him, cooling his forehead with a wet washcloth. At first he thought she was a ghost, then he felt guilty for thinking such a thought about his own mother. He couldn't tell if he'd been asleep. He touched his fingers to his eyes and found them swollen.

What was all that noise? she said. Were you having a nightmare?

What would we do if cars quit working? he said. He didn't know where his question had come from, but the grocery store was twenty minutes away. How would anyone buy things?

I guess we'd walk, said Mother.

But it's too far.

Horses. We could ride a horse.

You don't know how to ride a horse.

Just cause I'm a woman doesn't mean I can't figure it out.

You don't even have a horse, he said, his voice rising. No one does.

We'd trade in the car and get a horse instead.

What if there was a war and they shot all the horses and everything blew up and nothing worked and the army came to shoot us?

Hush now, said Mother.

There's not even a lock on my window.

She lifted her glass of buttermilk from Loren's bedside table and sipped from it. Buttermilk was the one thing in the refrigerator Loren didn't like. It was staining the sides of her glass. He wanted to go see if she was in her room sleeping in her bed too, if there were two of her.

Can I sleep in your bed tonight?

I feel like I want to sleep alone, she said.

He could sense the light brown of the peanut butter mixing in his stomach with the dark brown of the apple butter, turning white in reaction to his acids. He could use a separate blanket in her bed; they'd draw a line down the middle. She kept the door locked at night now, and he wondered if she slept at all.

I wouldn't mind your snoring. I could move my own bed into your room.

Why don't you just sleep with Luther. Luther doesn't snore.

Yes he does. He's just the same as you.

If we're the same, you'll be fine sleeping with him instead.

I don't mean you're the same as him. That's not what I meant at all.

He wanted to tell her he loved her more than me, but he couldn't say it. He imagined himself saying it. He tried to hear his voice, not just how it sounded inside his head, distorted by his skull, but the real thing. He thought of different ways to put the words. His brain was sweating with our names. I would have gone away. I never wanted him not to love her.

That's what you said, sweetie.

I don't know why I said it.

It's okay. It didn't hurt my feelings.

She turned out the light and left the room. When he was younger, she used to sing to him at night, to keep him from being scared. She'd sing folk songs, old Child ballads from her

Joan Baez songbook, and he would sing along: Matty Groves, House Carpenter, Mary Robinson. In all the songs, young girls died because men had hurt them. Some were sent to the gallows for crimes they didn't commit. Some drowned at sea; others fell ill and became ghosts, trapped indefinitely in limbo between earth and the next world. He considered that everything Mother had ever done to help him feel safe had only made him more afraid.

It won't matter about the lock on your window, I told him. They can blow the whole earth up all at once now. But don't worry about it; you won't know, because it'll happen so fast.

He shivered beneath his comforter and counted numbers to try to sleep. They scrolled quickly by, and he wished he could slow them down. If a bomb blew him up, he thought, he'd never know the date. Footsteps creaked through the walls, and he prayed for it not to be burglars. He was wide awake. Today could be the number on his grave. If the bomb blew, he wanted to spend his final living instant memorizing it, burning his headstone's numerals across his mind.

He dreamed he vomited jars and jars of pasta sauce, whole stewed tomatoes riding it like capsized lifeboats, but then it was just blood.

The next morning was the funeral, and Loren went to the bathroom to get ready. He was scared his suit would already be too small for him after two days' time, but it wasn't, although the belt was tight. He hated belts and pants in general. If Mother got to wear a suit, he thought, he should get to wear a dress. He'd have been ashamed to do it, and it made him admire his mother for her lack of care. Adults never had as much of a problem with shame as he had.

When he took off his pajama bottoms, he saw that his boils had grown worse.

That's the most disgusting thing I've ever seen, I told him.

The pustules looked like oily kernels of popcorn. I wanted to touch one and know if they were hot or cold.

What if they keep getting worse until I die?

I was the one that made them get worse. I doubt if I'll let them kill you, though.

Stop it, Luther, it's got nothing to do with you.

Why are they there, then? Did you put them there yourself?

It's hidradenitis suppurativa. It's completely natural.

That's about as ridiculous as that gender diphtheria business.

He stared fearfully into the bathroom mirror, wondering if the boils would cover his whole body. The doctor had said it was caused by sweat beneath his belt buckle. Losing weight would help. If he were a girl, he wouldn't have a buckle at all. If he were a girl, he wouldn't even have been fat. It was probably his own gender dysphoria causing him to overeat, because the condition was hereditary and would keep progressing until he died.

Stop trying to explain your problems like that, I told him. I was the one who caused it, and I couldn't kill you even if I wanted to. I'm not allowed, and anyway what would be the purpose of all that I'm doing if I wanted you to die?

What are you talking about?

It's complicated. It has to do with where your loyalties lie.

I don't have any loyalty to you. I hate you.

Things might change, though. Mother might be going away for a while.

Loren heard Mother stirring in the next room, so he finished putting his suit on and went to the living room, where Mother stood in the same black suit she'd worn to the viewing.

Are you going somewhere? he said.

To the funeral, Loren. You know that. I swan.

After the funeral, though.

Did somebody tell you I'm going somewhere?

Why were we in that driveway yesterday?

Luther's not somebody you should be listening to.

Just tell me where it is you're going to go.

Maybe to the grocery store, I guess. We're out of just about everything.

Loren went to the kitchen to make sure the stove eyes were off before we left, and then he checked the coffeemaker and the stove eyes again and the coffeemaker one more time and the stove eyes. Mother was going out the door, though, and he didn't want her to think he was eating. She hadn't even noticed. She was already sitting in the Chevette, staring blankly into space. Loren got in the car too, and she drove down the driveway and away. Her seat belt was in her free hand.

Put your seat belt on, said Loren. We're moving.

I was around back when cars didn't even have seat belts.

But cars have always had seat belts, since they were invented.

Really? Where were you when they passed the law?

How could they make cars without seat belts? Why would anyone do that?

There's things you ought to worry about more than seat belts, Loren.

Was she threatening him? Was she going somewhere, as I had said? Why would she consciously want her own son to worry?

Just forget I said that, Loren. I don't want you to be fretting all day and night. Everything's gonna turn out okay in the end.

The funeral was at the same Primitive Baptist Church with the same nameless valley spread out below us. The marquee read *Anger is a wind blowing out of the lamp*. I soared up to the rafters and beyond them to the summit ridge of the mountain, all the way to the lookout tower on Look Rock. No one noticed me there, and I descended again. Loren stood around like a half-inflated ball, nervous, because this was his first funeral, and he didn't know what he was supposed to do.

Don't worry, I said, I've been to lots of funerals.

No you haven't.

Yes I have.

No you haven't.

Yes I have. Don't worry about it.

Everyone was there, all the great-aunts, second cousins, friends from Mamaw's sewing group and knitting group and quilting group and crocheting group. Loren wondered if Mother would have this many friends too when she was Mamaw's age. He was continually pulling his pants lower to try to move his belt below his condition. The pallbearers were Cass, Papaw, Dusty, and a man barely old enough to be an adult. Loren had never seen him before, and apparently Mother hadn't, either. She stared into the back of that fourth pallbearer's head. She spent most of the whole ceremony staring into his head. She was liable to burn a hole into the back of his head from staring so hard at it. When the service was over, she went to Ruby and demanded to know who it was.

Somebody Cass knows from that turkey shoot.

The most important turkey shoot of the whole season?

Right, the one that's more important than the other ones.

You think I can't lift a coffin, then?

Why would you want to go touching coffins, Avery?

Why would you want to bury anybody at all? Why not let birds nibble out our guts on the side of the mountain?

I know you said don't tell you what you are no more, Avery, but whatever it is you think it is you are, you're not.

What's this little prick's name, anyway?

The turkey shoot kid?

The fourth pallbearer.

Gurney Flinchum.

So that's more respectable than I am?

Don't ask questions you don't like the answers to.

I could lift that coffin all by myself, Ruby.

What's the point of that if it's already in the dirt?

And why not Loren? What about him?

I paid for the coffin anyway. I guess I've got a say in who touches it and who don't.

Ruby, as soon as that money comes in I'm paying my share and you know it.

I wouldn't want that, Avery. Can't you ever accept some charity?

If that's charity then you can suck my asshole.

It's your condition causes you to say things like that.

Daddy says it all the time and you don't raise a finger.

So you want to be more like Daddy? That's what this is all about? There's a admirable goal. Anyway the payment came through this morning. I can deduct the coffin part from your check if that's what you want. But I don't know if Mommy would want to lie in rest in a coffin that you'd helped pay for. I mean I'm not being mean; I'm just saying.

Mother crossed the churchyard parking lot to where a few of the men were gathered around their trucks. Loren prayed she wouldn't make a scene, because scenes made him nervous. Papaw would eventually make one himself anyway, so Loren saw no need for Mother to make one, but I figured she might as well shake things up a bit by making a scene before anyone else could. She marched straight up to the fourth pallbearer and tapped him on the shoulder.

You're pretty strong, she said, aren't you?

Gurney Flinchum stopped talking to Cass and Dusty about turkeys and turned to Mother. She was about six inches shorter than any of them. Gurney looked frightening to Loren, but Dusty was the one he was most scared of. Dusty was one of those pervasive people who just pervades everything. Everywhere his signs had been hammered into the ground. Thousands upon thousands of men would come all the way from Knoxville to live in his houses, he said. He must have thought he had the whole county figured out. He didn't understand Mother one bit, though. Gurney probably understood her even less, but he was a stranger, and Loren was expecting him to fall right back out of their lives as quickly as he had entered.

Why don't you arm wrestle me? she said.

What would be the point of that? said Cass.

This is between me and Gurney. Gurney, are your arms too sore from carrying that coffin to arm wrestle me?

They ain't sore. I just don't see the point, though.

Then I guess you and Cass are a lot alike. Neither one of you can see the point. I understand now why you're friends. I know this is a funeral, a tragic time for all involved and if there's only one thing that can be expected in this sad time, it's to show respect to the deceased, but I don't know the deceased that well, in fact the deceased told me I was an abomination and I haven't been in much contact with her these past nine years, so why don't you humor me a moment and help me prove a point.

Gurney looked at Cass and Dusty, who both shrugged, and then he unbuttoned the cuff of his shirt and rolled up the sleeve and put his elbow on the hood of his Chevrolet truck. Most of the other people were watching too. Loren was watching, and I was certainly watching. Mother didn't bother doing anything about her sleeves. The suit was already dirty anyway, and I doubt she planned to wear it again anytime soon. One two three go, she said. Immediately the strain on both of them showed. Their faces tightened and grew red. Neither arm moved. Loren was terrified of what might happen. The danger of games was that the game could be lost. People were watching, and Mother stood to be humiliated. She might prove she was incapable of being a man. Maybe Gurney had something to lose too, but Gurney didn't seem to care.

He's not trying, I said.

Yes he is, Loren said, they're tied.

Mother and I are tied too, but that doesn't mean we're both trying.

Trying to do what? What would you be trying?

He was the stupidest person in the world, and I don't know why I continued caring about him so much. What was in it for me? What made me want him to succeed? Whatever it is I'm good at, I wanted him to be just as good, so we could be good at it together. If that meant causing mischief, tearing things down, abandoning them, setting ourselves against the world, then fine, Loren should have been willing to do that too. We could have been having a lot of fun together. Mother was miserable. She wasn't any fun, and that wasn't what Loren wanted to hear. I guess he wanted to make his body as uncomfortable as hers, but what was the fun of that? I flew above him to show him the opposite of what he was doing to himself, or what she was doing to him by being a part of his life at all. I soared through the trees at hundreds of miles an hour, but Loren ignored me, focusing on the arm wrestling. It had gone on for more than half a minute. Mother's arm looked like it would give out any second. Loren had the sense that Cass and Dusty were rooting against Mother. Why would they go against their own family? He was glad Papaw wasn't watching. Papaw was by the grave, arguing with the preacher. They'd given Mamaw a grave that didn't have a view of the valley. Loren looked toward the church, and when he looked back, Gurney's arm was pressed flat to the hood of the truck. Gurney had lost, and Mother looked crazed. It didn't seem appropriate to congratulate her. He tugged at his belt. His feet hurt in the black dress shoes; next time he'd go barefoot. Was it bad to think about other funerals? He didn't want to cause anyone to die. He closed his eyes and shut his brain so no one's name would come to mind. He tried to think about Jesus to keep anything else from happening, because Jesus was already dead. The faces of the graves gleamed on the hillside from steeple to sun, and Loren catalogued the names and numbers, bold and capital, that were carved in stone.

Papaw looked into the grave and said, Well, there won't be any more Mamaw.

Eventually everyone meandered into the church. Only certain kinds of flowers were displayed; you couldn't pick just any old flower for funerals. Papaw continued arguing with the preacher, his arms in the air.

Don't sorry me. Everybody done put their hundred-dollar clothes on.

You've had that suit since 1962, said Ruby.

Money looked the same then as it does now.

They had those buffalo heads, said Cass.

You weren't even there.

I was there just like you were.

Your eyes was still closed.

You're thinking of mice.

And that cake looks like a wedding cake, not a funeral cake.

Ruby threw her arms into the air too. I guess I should be glad I can even talk, she said, looking around at the general murmur in the room.

Loren went to the table and chose a piece of cake and ate it quickly so no one would think, There he goes again, of all the times. Ruby saw him and used him as an escape from Papaw.

You're so lucky. Everything's ahead of you. So many places to go.

You go more places than we do, Loren said.

Who's we? You don't mean that little thing of yours again.

Me and Mother, I mean.

She nodded. I wish I was in your place.

Of course she doesn't really want to be fat like you, I told him.

That's my piece of cake you took, Papaw barked. Give it here.

Loren laid the plastic fork on the saucer, but it wouldn't balance, so he stuck it into the cake upright.

Good God, said Papaw, don't eat no more of it.

Loren tried to hold on, to hand it over the right way, but he let go at the same time as Papaw. Cake bounced down the front of Loren's suit, icing his pants leg from the knee down to the cuff hem.

That was your fault, not mine, said Loren.

Just had to have one more bite, didn't you? I give your mama eighty dollars to buy that suit. Things is more expensive in the husky section, cause they're bigger.

Papaw noticed suddenly how the whole room was watching him shout, and he got louder and said, Listen up. Ain't nobody better die no more. I can't afford suits for every damn funeral. He headed toward Mother, digging his wallet out of his pocket as he walked, then pulling cards out of the leather folds. Ruby was maneuvering through the crowd too as Papaw shouted, Take it all. Go sell it to all them Japs down in Monroe County.

I don't know what you mean, said Mother.

Won't even be the money left to plant me right. You'll plant me in a pine box.

Father, said Ruby, I want you could be a little quieter.

My daddy use to say you can want in one hand and shit in the other.

That pine box might do you a world of good.

I don't even know what the hell it meant. How could you want in a damn hand.

Loren wandered through the conversations. Will not even care for her own yard. What possesses her to drive a Chevrolet I don't know. Likely did not eat sufficient eggs as a child not that I blame poor Birdie. Drives into that city up there you couldn't pay me the money to go.

The old ladies fell into a hush whenever Loren approached. He got tired of it and went outside, where the sky had grown plump with gray clouds that hovered in the distance, shedding their mist, threatening to irrigate Mamaw right back up out of her grave. The funeral couldn't last forever, and eventually we got to leave. Mother drove home a different way, past one of Dusty's new developments. The sign said *Dustin Drake, Developer*. Dusty built subdivisions out of farms and woods; he'd moved here just two months ago when he married Ruby, and he was excited because of all the land. Maybe he could develop the whole mountain. Dead trees lined the new street of the neighborhood we were driving past. Power poles were being erected. Loren played with his seat belt and unfastened it.

Why does Dusty build subdivisions?

Where else would people live?

I've read books where people walk to everything.

That sounds nice.

Why isn't it like that here?

Things used to be safer than they are now.

What kinds of things?

Just things in general. Be happy you don't have to walk. Kids in poor countries still walk all over the place. That's why we have cars.

Aren't you going to make me put my seat belt on?

We're going twenty-five miles an hour.

You can get killed at twenty-five.

So put your seat belt on.

You have to make me do it.

Put it on, then. I'm making you.

I don't want to.

You just said you did.

You're not doing it right, though.

Then just don't talk to me! Just look out your window and shut up.

Loren didn't see how everything worked so well. He knew he wasn't supposed to be nervous about what would happen five years in the future, but he couldn't help it. He wanted Mother just to say it was okay, to pat him on the head and say relax, you'll know what to do, you'll figure things out, you'll find the answers, but she wouldn't say any of these things. As we pulled up to the house I reminded him of when times were better, when he was younger and smaller and Mother's condition wasn't so far along, and she wore her hair longer and shaved her legs and her voice wasn't as deep and she hadn't started wearing her chest binder. She would take him down to Roulette Spring to pick blackberries as if the two of them were friends of the same age. They'd walk together through the thorns until they had enough blackberries to make pies all year round, and then they'd lie together in tall grass and the sun would tan them together. In Loren's memory that was how the whole year had been. He'd had a vague sense that Mother was unhappy, but for the most part she was happy. He would put violets in his hair, which had been long and blond, and he imagined people wouldn't know he was a boy. But then they'd made fun of him in kindergarten, and Mother had cut his hair, which had turned brown in response. Things had been bad ever since. Loren's good memories seemed like a curse. It would be nicer to remember when things had been worst of all. He tried to think of such a time. Things would certainly be worse in the future, and if he could only remember the future, he might have been able to take solace in remembering memories, as everyone else on the planet seemed to do. He wandered the house thinking these thoughts. It was hard to torment someone who cared about only one thing in the entire world, but Mother decided to help me. She knew the best thing after a time of extreme personal loss was to get right back to work, so she went outside and started chopping down the hedges. She wasn't going to let anyone criticize her yard. She hacked away at the forsythias, which were dead, and the junipers and hollies, which appeared to be alive. She hacked at too many branches at once; leaves fluttered down but wood remained. Her bandanna was soon drenched in sweat.

You're not cutting any of the branches, Loren said.

You think I'm not getting anything done? Useless woman. Can't clean up her own yard.

Loren needed to think of something to say so that he wouldn't just be staring at her, so he thought of a lie: I remember what that dream was about.

That dumb thing about the horses and cars?

You died, and I couldn't remember what you sounded like.

You remembered horses, but my death slipped your mind.

We have to buy a tape recorder so I can record your voice.

We can't afford something like that, Loren.

You keep talking about getting a bunch of money.

Just listen close to what I say, and you'll remember and stop talking about dying.

If you die, you'll have been dead half my life before I'm twenty.

We'll see how well you remember my voice then after I'm gone.

It already sounds different than it did last year.

My voice? she said.

Uh-huh. I don't mind, though.

She cut a small bush down completely with one snap of the shears.

It took that bush nine years to grow that big, said Loren.

How would you know how long it's been growing, anyway?

You said you planted it when I was born.

Well I said a lot of things.

Mother surveyed what she'd done to the bushes and breathed carefully as if to say, You did this, this was you, and he wondered if she wanted to prune him too, so that the rest of him would grow back the right way. It occurred to Loren that there should be a separate word for how she was staring into the dead chestnut tree, the way of staring where you weren't even trying to see the thing before you. It made Loren want to cry, but he blinked it back.

Are we going to Ruby's for Easter tomorrow, to dye eggs?

I might let you go on alone, she said.

What do you mean? How could you not go color eggs?

Well, you asked if I was, so I said no.

We've colored eggs at Ruby's every Easter since forever.

She lives at a different house now. We'll see what happens.

What's going on, Mother? Why are you being so weird?

I'm a weird person, Loren.

No you're not, you're a normal person.

Would you be sad if I died?

Of course I would.

I don't think I'm very sad about Mamaw.

It's different. Mamaw was older.

Oh, sweetie, said Mother, suddenly hugging him tight. She looked desperate to say something, on the verge of tears. Something blocked her from talking. It never occurred to Loren that that something was me. I started wanting to do something nice for him. At the same time, I started to worry she was about to renege on the bet, and that he'd run away with her.

Do you trust me? she said.

He nodded, frightened of her tone.

You're just gonna have to keep trusting me, then.

Her grip was the tightest of anyone who had ever touched

him. How many people had touched him before? It was at least five people. He wished she'd quit; his shirt was getting wet. He thought about the box of cookies in the fruit basket. She let go of him and resumed cutting. Soon the house was naked to the wind and road and trees, and Loren sat alone in it eating cookies, reading a book in which people aged more quickly the higher on a mountain they lived, so that every moment was more valuable. He thought about what he could do to make himself trustworthy enough to confide in. He lied sometimes about how much food he'd eaten. Mother probably knew that. He figured she was dying to tell him what was going on. If only he could stop being secretive and admit he felt the same way so they could truly understand each other. On the other hand, it might make her feel even worse, because she'd know she had passed her problems on to him. No, she'd understand he didn't blame her. None of it was her fault. He felt grateful to be alive at all. If he weren't so secretive and selfish, he'd have thanked her by now for giving birth to him.

That's the dumbest thing I've ever heard, I said. I never thanked anyone for creating me.

You say everything's the dumbest thing you've ever heard.

That's because everything you say gets dumber each time. Anyway, I didn't ask her to bring me into the world.

She didn't bring you into the world.

Yes she did.

No she didn't.

Yes she did.

And that was the last thing I said to him, because I too was bound by the terms of the wager, and it was time to abide, and wait. Loren went to bed and lay awake most of the night. When he awoke late the next morning, Mother was gone. The Chevette wasn't in the driveway, and she wasn't in the bathroom or under her bed or in the closet. Loren looked in the laundry room and in the kitchen cabinets, in her cedar chest where she'd saved her dresses for Loren in case he'd been a girl. He unfolded a yellow one and held it up to himself. How would he color eggs without Mother? The weeds were getting high; soon someone would have to mow the grass. Maybe Mother had gone to buy a new car that didn't have so much pollen on it, or she was out rescuing turtles from the road. He didn't mind not being with her if it was just a few minutes, but it had already been more than a few minutes. He looked under the house in the crawlspace, with the skillets. Coming back inside, he found a note on the porch weighted by a stone.

Call Ruby, it said. *555-6110, she'll bring you to color eggs.*

Loren went to the phone and looked at it for about fifteen minutes. He hated using phones. People always thought he sounded like a girl on the phone, and it made him mad, which didn't make any sense, but neither did anything else about him. Mother had said it would get better when his voice changed, but he didn't want that to happen, either. He supposed Ruby would recognize his voice, and he didn't need to say *this is Loren*. If he said it, it might insult her, because she was family, but if he didn't say it, she might think he was just some girl. Everything in life was so terribly complicated; he felt angry at Mother for leaving him here to make these decisions by himself. He felt alone. He hadn't yet noticed that I had abandoned him too. If he had thought my name, I wouldn't have responded. I just didn't have that option. Call me malicious and spiteful and jealous, but I'm honorable, and I intended to keep my word. Finally Loren dialed Ruby's telephone number, praying she'd be the one to answer and not Dusty or any of his wicked nephews or worst of all Eli.

Hello? said Dusty after six rings.

Hi this is Loren is Ruby there?

Oh, hi Lorn. I thought you were some girl.

Loren didn't respond, because it wasn't a question.

Well, I'll go get her, said Dusty.

As Loren waited, he thought of the things Ruby might tell him. Mother was at Ruby's already. Mother was on her way to Ruby's from visiting Mamaw's grave. Mother loved dyeing eggs with Loren, and she might have wanted a head start. Or maybe something had gone entirely wrong with the plan to dye eggs. Maybe Ruby had cancer. That would be terrible, but it would be better than something happening to Mother. Maybe it was Mamaw. They couldn't dye eggs so soon after Mamaw's death. The whole family was supposed to be in mourning, wearing black and ruminating on the sadness of Mamaw's passing.

Hello? said Ruby.

Hi, Ruby, it's me.

Hello? she said again.

This is Loren.

Oh, Lorn, I didn't recognize your voice.

Mother left a note for me to call you.

There's all these girls calling from Knoxville, what with Eli here.

It's not a girl, it's just me.

That Eli is a real lady-killer.

What do you mean?

It's just a figure of speech, Lorn.

Ruby was always using figures of speech when she didn't want to answer people's questions. But he hadn't asked a question yet at all. Maybe she didn't know Loren was supposed to call.

I guess your mama told you she had to go up the mountain for a few days. It's nothing for you to worry about.

Is that a figure of speech too?

Is what a figure of speech?

Up the mountain.

What kind of figure of speech would that be?

You made it sound like she died.

Nobody's died around here. Well, you know what I mean.

I don't know what you mean at all.

Top of the World. She's decided to check herself in for a few days, till her head can get better. It's nothing to worry about. It'll be fun, because you can stay with us for a bit.

Mother wouldn't leave without telling me.

Why would I lie to you?

I'm not trying to say you're lying.

I figured she would have told you already.

Maybe Ruby was telling the truth, but Loren sincerely doubted it.

I'm gonna send Cass over to pick you up, so get your stuff.

What kind of stuff do I need?

Lorn, come on now, you're not helpless.

Loren had heard of people who just disappeared. Their children woke up one morning to find them gone, because they were too selfish to provide explanations. Loren had never had the chance to ask Mother whether she'd wanted him to be a girl or a boy, whether she'd wanted him to be born at all—but it was too early to worry he'd never see her again. Maybe she just wanted to know what the rest of the family would do to him. She always said they couldn't wait to get their hands on him. It wasn't that they cared; they just wanted to prove they were right and Mother was wrong. They said if he was a boy, which he was, he needed to go outside and play, and he needed to eat less, but they weren't interesting people when all they did was try to make him eat less. Loren thought of hiding in the woods when Cass came to pick him up. The fact that Ruby and Cass and Papaw wanted him to lose weight made him not even want to. He could prove they were useless by doing the opposite of whatever they said. He started to make his way into the woods, but already his plan was flawed, because they could still talk to him in his head. It was almost worse than the real thing, because they were smarter in his head than in real life. It was enough to make Loren want to cut off his head, but that was just what they wanted him to do. The red berries that grew on the forest floor could kill him; he thought of ending his life that way, too. In the past he'd been scared that a bird might drop one into his mouth. Mother might think he'd swallowed it on purpose; then she'd swallow a berry too so they could die together. The romance of this thought had brought him to tears at the time, and he was proud of himself for having overcome his fear of death by berries; there were different things to fear now, like Cass's truck, speaking to Cass on the drive, speaking to him on Ruby's patio without Mother. Loren faced these fears and came out of the woods and found that the truck itself was a legitimate fear, because it had arrived, but speaking to Cass was an unnecessary fear, because Cass was silent the whole way.

There you are, said Ruby, when he arrived. Happy Easter.

Ruby lived in a brand-new split-foyer house right on the main road. Mother had said no one's house was nice enough for the viewing, but it wasn't true; Ruby's house was plenty nice. She wasn't like the rest of the family. She didn't believe in the powers of vegetables. She subscribed to *Southern Living* and *Reader's Digest* and intended to better herself. For the most part, the bettering of herself was already done. There were always finishing touches to put on things, though. She would move her jars of seashells around depending on where that month's *Southern Living* said they should go. Her bathroom was bigger than Loren's bedroom, and it had had a framed poster from *The Ten Commandments* hanging over the towel rack until Eli broke the glass in the frame. Eli was a malicious devil who didn't believe in Tradition. For Ruby, Tradition took the place of the powers of vegetables; that was why Easter and the other holidays were always celebrated at her house. On holidays people could do the same things as the last year, remembering the pleasures they'd had that year but also enjoying the unique delights of the new year. Everyone was so glad to be there. The sun shone brightly on Ruby and Cass and Papaw and Dusty and the nephews and now Loren as they sat on the brand-new deck that stretched halfway across the back of her house and all the way around the side, above the driveway.

So you've finely drove her to the loony bin, said Papaw.

Hush now, said Ruby, I already explained him it's not his fault none.

I tole her the day you was born you'd send her a-packin.

I got you an Easter basket, Lorn. We're fresh out of candy, though.

Because a your cone head. You come out your head was a cone head. You ast me you tore up the inside of her with that cone head course I wasn't the one chose to do it.

Pa, will you shut up or make some sense? said Cass.

Who the hell's side are you on here, peckerwood?

There's no sides, said Ruby, this is Easter. It's a together time.

Creed and Shay and Millard, Dusty's little nephews, were continuing their Easter egg hunt in the yard. Loren strung a thread of pink Easter grass around his hand, wishing it were a wand to make people tell the truth, and to make them levitate against their will. Dusty looked at Cass, who looked at Papaw, who looked at Ruby, the four of them forming an impenetrable square.

She just needed some time to herself, said Ruby. You know her mama just passed.

It's your mother too, said Loren. You're not to yourself.

Avery and me aren't quite the same, I suppose.

Only thing Avery's the same as, snorted Papaw, is herself.

Loren could look down from Ruby's yard and see the clouded eyes of passing drivers. He could tell in those eyes whether they were headed out for the papers or embarking on a journey across the continent. He listed in his mind the ways he could miss school the next day: he could get sick from salmonella in the Easter eggs, the school could flood, the governor could visit from Nashville which would call off classes, or Miss Rathbone could have a stroke. That last one wouldn't work, because Mr. Ownby would hire a substitute teacher. Dread moved in waves through Loren's blood. He'd expected Eli to be out in the yard breaking everyone's eggs, and Dusty cheering his son on all the while. Eli was probably with his mother, though, which made Loren feel sorry for himself. Mother hadn't even bought him an Easter basket. Maybe she wanted him eating less chocolate, but he hardly ate chocolate at all; chocolate was one of his least favorite desserts.

Thirty, Millard yelled.

Thirty-two, said Creed.

Millard stole an egg from Creed's basket and threw it at Creed's head.

Now you just got thirty-one, loser.

Loren floated above his chair and breathed as slowly as he could. Someone's one-eared candy rabbit on the picnic table rose too, so he bit its flesh to calm his stomach. He bit again, and the whole sweet skull of pure milk chocolate died inside his mouth.

Thank you for the Easter basket, he told Ruby.

Why don't you go play now. Go out in the yard and have some fun.

I'm having fun right here. This is a lot of fun.

Dusty and Ruby tried to think of street names for their new development. Ruby wanted to call it Saviordale—He Forgives Drive, Only Begotten Boulevard—but Dusty said that that was stupid; he preferred Riverlake, although it was miles from the water.

Where is this place you're talking about? said Loren.

Hasn't Avery told you yet about Saviordale? said Ruby.

She wouldn't have told no Saviordale, said Dusty, cause it's Riverlake.

Explain me how can you have such a thing as a riverlake?

It don't stop being a river just cause lakes, Dusty explained.

I'm saying a thing is either one thing or the other, and you can't make it not.

Look here, Ruby, said Papaw, he's sayin to you a river already is a lake.

It's a lake that's a lake, she cried, or I'm the queen of France!

Then what do they to dam it up for if it ain't a lake?

The neighborhood is in a dale, Daddy, it's not in a riverlake.

I'll river your damn lake. Where's them eggs?

Loren wished he'd kept quiet about Mother's absence; he could live alone. People would feel sorry for him, and that would be nice. He looked toward Chilhowee Mountain. He could see Look Rock Tower, and he tried to make out the hospital but couldn't. It was probably on the other side. It was probably invisible to him forever. He gauged the distance from Ruby's to the foot of the mountain to be about three miles. He was considering walking it when the family ran out of things to say, causing Easter to be over, so that Loren was whisked away to Cass's house, much closer to the mountain, on Indian Warpath Road.

Don't worry none, said Cass, as they drove to the house, there's a bedroom where you can sleep in. I got tools and such in the garage you can fool around with if you get bored.

Loren realized Cass was trying to comfort him, but he didn't feel grateful. Tools were the last thing he needed right now, and Cass should have known that, or at least come up with additional ways to make Loren feel better. Cass wasn't much of a talker, though, and fell permanently silent for the rest of the drive. As they came to the house, a cloud approached the top of the mountain, and consumed Mother in moisture. How long do you think we'll stay here? Loren thought, but there wasn't anyone else in his head anymore.

Cass lived with his girlfriend, Delia, in a custard-yellow house set back about two hundred feet from the dead-end road. It was a split-foyer, like Ruby's, but the house was the furthest thing from Ruby's that Loren could imagine. The weedy yard was littered with engine parts, causing the whole property to smell like oil. The gutter was disconnected from the roof due to the weight of soggy leaves that had collected in it over several years' time. The bottom half of the house wasn't painted; it was exposed gray cinder blocks. The windows of the black garage door had been painted over.

Go in the garage there while I make sure things inside's set up right.

You don't have to do anything special, said Loren.

Just get yourself in that garage there and find something to do.

But nothing in the garage was doable; it was only car parts and boxing gloves and about two dozen guns and a swimsuit calendar hanging on pegboard. He stood listlessly on the concrete looking for a place to sit, hoping Cass wouldn't be mad at him for finding nothing to do. My departure meant he had to interact with other people now. In worrying about Mother he'd forgotten that I too could have saved him from having to talk to Cass. I was second-best, so he ignored me and braced himself for the interaction. We could have done it together, but he wouldn't think my name. Mother was winning the wager, and I felt jealous and alone. I hoped Cass would beat Loren up and leave him whimpering and broken in the garage. Loren had one-sixth of Cass's blood, and there was a good chance he'd grow up to look just like Cass—I wished that on him too—but all Cass did when he came back out was arm wrestle him.

Arm wrestle me. I ain't gonna hurt you. I'll give you a prize if you win.

Cass walked over and pressed his elbow onto a plank that lay across some RC Cola crates, grinding the red joint into place. Put her down, he said to Loren, who meekly placed his elbow on the wood. I ain't gonna hurt you. I'm family. You ready then?

I don't know if I want to arm wrestle.

Live at your own house if you want to get what you want.

With our two strengths together, we could have beat him. I alone could have obliterated him. I could have scorched him off the face of the earth. But I watched Loren's knuckles hit the plank. Cass held his fist in the air and grinned and drank and said, Hot damn, I am so good, as Loren rubbed his knuckles in pain.

Go again, said Cass. You ain't got your prize yet.

There's no prize. Tell me what the prize is.

This is what drove your mama crazy—you won't do what folks say.

Mother's not crazy.

Where is she then?

Loren thought about that. Mother either cared about his welfare, or she didn't. If she did, she'd never left, and he was dreaming; if she didn't, she was insane, and belonged away from humanity at Top of the World for the rest of her life. At this moment, he wished I would come. It was still early on, and he hadn't completely forgotten me in favor of Mother. Where could I have gone? Help me, he thought, not connecting my disappearance with hers, failing to realize there could even be that much deception in the world. Ready set go, said Cass, and Loren pushed as hard as he could. Maybe, he thought, I'd be here pushing too, if he showed me how badly he wanted me there. Then he imagined my telling him he was better off without her, and now he could lose weight and look like me again, and the idea scared him so much that he strained against Cass's arm alone for seven whole breaths before he was beaten.

Now Lorn, look here, you're not trying right.

There's no wrong way to try. You just try.

There's a wrong way for everything, and you know it.

That was exactly the lesson Loren needed to learn. The fact that I couldn't have said it better myself was a minor comfort to me as I ripped myself from Loren's world and left him alone in the control of Papaw, Cass, and Ruby, none of whom even believed in me, which I hoped would make Loren mad, which gave me some confidence that in the end I might win the wager and gain control of Loren for the rest of his life.

Well, your mama did okay at it.

I want to go home.

You're bein thisaway cause of your girl's name.

Loren's not a girl's name, though.

The hell it's not. Listen to it.

Your name's a girl's name, not mine.

Cass thought about it. No my name ain't; it's Cass.

Name another boy in the world called Cass.

Cass took a minute before he answered, I'll tell you a secret.

You don't know any secrets.

I was a sissy too, just like you. Your mama used to beat me up.

You're older than she is. You would have been bigger.

She didn't like sissies. But now she's jealous of me.

What would she be jealous of someone like you for?

Cass chuckled. That's a different secret, he said.

The pork chops Delia was cooking smelled like sour armpits. Cass followed the smell inside, and Loren followed Cass. Delia wore an apron around her waist and had tied back her jet-black hair. Her dark skin and black eyes reminded Loren of a gypsy's, though he'd never seen a real gypsy. Like with the

Indians, the government had given them homes to get them out of everybody's way, and they weren't around anymore. Cass had found Delia at the turkey shoot like everything else. She was seventeen years old, and she served from a pot of pinto beans like a timid doe. There were rules; you had to sit a certain way. Delia didn't say a word as she served the pork chops with corn, carrots, and peas.

Put your napkin in your lap, Cass said. Didn't Avery teach you manners?

We don't eat sit-down meals much.

Talkin back. There's manners. Damn Avery manners.

Loren wanted to yell at Cass, but it would seem out of character, and people made fun of him when he did things he didn't usually do. He wanted to ask where Delia came from. He had no idea what a turkey shoot even was. Did they shoot real turkeys, or skeet that looked like turkeys? Whatever they did was fun, because Cass went back again and again. Did they shoot anything at all, or was it a secret code for something? Why had Mother wanted to go too? Loren thought he might never know the answers to his questions. He ate his pork chop and nibbled at his carrots and left the peas alone and pushed his plate aside.

Hey, Cass said, you didn't eat your peas.

I don't really like peas.

He didn't want it to sound like an insult, so he turned to Delia and said, The rest was really good, though.

Delia was clawing hers slowly with a fork, pausing after every bite. Them peas is gonna be good too, said Cass.

You can have mine if you want, then.

You're gonna eat them peas, big guy.

I'll throw up if I try to eat them.

All of a sudden he was worried; Cass didn't seem to understand. Delia's hands were folded in her lap as she stared at her plate.

If you do, you'll eat the throw-up too. Cass stood, the table at his waist, and pointed his fork at Loren. Let's see you eat some.

I'm allergic. I break out in hives.

Peas don't cause hives. You're a bullshit liar.

I had to go to the hospital once, I swear to God.

You'll swear to my belt on your ass.

Delia gripped her paper napkin, half smiling. She looked like she was being given what she wanted. Loren shoveled a spoonful of peas into his mouth. Immediately he began to gag. He swallowed water to wash them down like pills; that way he could barely taste them.

Please, I need another glass of water.

Avery teach you how to use a faucet?

Loren didn't understand why Cass was so interested in him. He wished Mother hadn't ever told any of her family she'd had a son. He could have locked himself in the closet when visitors came. Cass never would have figured it out.

He managed to drink the rest of his peas from his plate. The sun was setting. He asked to be excused and went to a spare room that was decorated with NASCAR posters and posters of country singers, particularly Reba McEntire. He felt Reba McEntire's many eyes looking down on him as he read some of the magazines lying around the room. Gun magazines revealed nothing about turkey shoots, and neither did fishing magazines. There wasn't a magazine for just turkey shoots, or if there was, Cass couldn't afford a subscription. Out in the front yard Cass fired a gun at tin cans, and Loren jumped at every ricochet.

Delia opened his door to say goodnight. Is this normal? Loren asked her.

Yeah, she said shyly. Guns is normal, I guess.

Are bullets expensive?

He took all of your grandma's when she died.

I wouldn't have thought she'd have had bullets.

Well, said Delia, shrugging. Have you ever got shot?

Loren shook his head. Have you?

Out in the woods. This once. It spreads real slow through you.

What do you mean? Who was it that shot you?

It was them Indians with that war paint, but it was a dream, though.

What kind of Indian? Why did they do it?

I guess they're just Indians. Say, is it true about your mama?

Is what true about her? Do you know her?

Why she went off to the hospital or whatever thing.

Why did she? What do you mean?

I'm saying is it true, or is it not true?

I guess it's true, said Loren.

Well I'll be goddamned, it's true.

Delia wasn't his family and would have no reason to lie. She reminded him of one of Mother's girlfriends from up in Knoxville back when she went places. Knoxville was a big city where they understood more things. Mother had said it was good they lived close enough to Knoxville for her to drive there, or she'd have killed herself. That was back when Loren was young and no one believed he'd remember what was said to him. They'd said all kinds of things around him, and though he'd forgotten most of those things by now, he had a general intuitive sense that they'd been said, and that sense told him not to speak to Delia about anything besides guns. Soon she'd be gone from his life like all of Cass's girls, but Cass would stay forever. He looked at the clock every few moments and hoped it would be bedtime soon, so he could wake up and everything would be over.

But the next morning it wasn't over; it was the day for measurements in gym class. Miss Rathbone had the class follow Mr. Mashburn, the coach of the pee-wee football team, to the gym. He counted on his fingers as he spoke. We got to measure yuns fat percentage, yuns weight, yuns sit-ups, yuns push-ups. It was a new country-wide order straight from President Reagan. The President wanted to see how East Tennessee measured up to the other states. On the bottom bleacher lay a plastic implement with open pincers like pruning shears. Leland went first, and Mr. Mashburn hooked the claw to the skin of his arm. Eleven, he said to Eli, who held the clipboard. Leland stepped onto the scale, where he stood until Mr. Mashburn yelled out, Ninety-one. He snapped and snapped the claws until it was Loren's turn to let the plastic weapon sink into the folds of his skin.

Ow, he said, that hurts.

Didn't seem to hurt nobody else.

He wondered if his fat was more sensitive than theirs, and he forgot to be nervous about the number until Mr. Mashburn said, Lordy, lordy, lordy.

It was thirty-nine. Laughter that he couldn't hear coursed through him. Maybe the other kids didn't care what his number was. He had cared about their numbers, so he couldn't imagine that they weren't paying attention to his, which was twice as high as anyone else's. He wanted to know what that number meant, but he knew better than to ask what it was a measurement of. They'd say, How fat you are, or, How much you eat. He had a good understanding of how their minds worked. If he were thin and someone else were fat, he'd excel at making fun of that person for being fat. He'd come up with the funniest, most devastating things about fatness.

As they jogged the gym's perimeter, Loren thought of sneaking out, finding the principal, and asking if he knew what was truly going on in this gym. The principal was in charge of the whole school, and he was supposed to see things wisely and clearly. Before Loren could act, though, it was time for math, where he learned nothing he didn't already know, and then school was over and he rode the bus to Cass's house, where he found a plate of two dozen chocolate rumballs waiting on the kitchen counter.

Have one, Cass said. They're good.

He and Papaw were sitting in the living room watching TV. It startled Loren to see them there together, just sitting quietly, not fighting.

Is Mother back? he asked.

Do you hate me now? said Cass.

He figured Cass was talking to Papaw, not to him. But Cass continued, saying, I'm a terrible person. His voice was distant and sad.

No you're not. I don't hate anyone.

There was a commercial for lawn mowers and one for deck sealant. Cass chewed the edges of his ham sandwich and swallowed lumps of crust. He was looking particularly revolting, with his shirt off and his bandanna around his head. All Loren could focus on was his massive, apelike chest. He was horrified to think he might look like that too someday. Cass had a bit of a gut himself but managed to keep his fat confined to that one part of his body. Loren's body stored fat in every possible place, from his forehead to his toes. If he ever lost weight, the skin of his forehead and everywhere else would probably sag and grow wrinkled like an old woman's.

An ad for Top of the World came on and said, Depression is a curable illness, and Cass laughed sarcastically and said, Yeah right, they've got it all figured out.

You don't know, said Papaw, you ain't never tried to cure it.

You depressed or somethin, old man? Don't come weepin to me.

You're the one ain't never maired yet.

You ain't neither, no more. Can't use that one on me now.

Cure up your surliness and the girls'd be on you again.

You and her didn't even sleep in the same bed.

We ain't cavemen, Cass, we don't need each other for heat. We got that England stove. You're as bad as them Church of God people. That cross thing. Singin their songs.

The hospital looked like a nice tranquil place where calm people could watch the sun setting over the Cumberland Plateau. They could see the hawks circling over Maryville and they could see the house where Loren stood now. Looking at the television, he supposed he was looking at himself, and he wondered where he'd been when the scene was filmed. He repeated the phone number from the screen to himself over and over, making sure not to move his lips so that no one would know he was memorizing it. Meanwhile Cass and Papaw argued about asparagus. Papaw said asparagus got the cavities out of your bowels, but Cass said asparagus had got the cavities there in the first place and filled them with rot. What the good of the asparagus was, one of them said, was in your head. When they both turned to look at Loren at the same time, Loren knew they were talking about Mother. He didn't see how Mother could want to be anything resembling a man when Cass and Papaw were around. They switched the focus of their argument to lima beans and then chickens, which as far as they could tell had no powers except for strength. You needed a lot of meat to make you strong, and Mother had eaten too much meat. She'd gotten strong without using vegetables to develop the other parts of her body, such as her gut and her mind.

I supposed you could say it's my fault, said Papaw, since I raised her, but I give her carrots just like I give you, and she never eat none, and you turned out good. That's the reason to have three kids in the first place is so one turns out good.

Papaw glanced at Loren as if to say Mother had been wrong not to have three kids herself. She'd caused Loren to turn out wrong by having just one of him.

I don't mean nothing by that now, Lorn, it's just words.

Now a good piece a liver is what makes you strong, said Cass.

That's what Avery ate her whole life was liver.

But a liver ain't chicken, and you said chicken.

Well a chicken has got a blame liver, ain't it?

How come we don't eat it then? How come all we eat is cow livers? What's wrong with the liver of a goat or a fish liver?

Loren went to the telephone in the kitchen and dialed the number. He planned to make his voice sound like a man's, but he got nervous and hung up after three rings. Then he picked the phone up and dialed again.

Top of the World, said an old woman. Outpatient.

Hello, Loren stammered, I'm trying to find if someone's there.

Most likely it's confidential.

But I'm her son.

Loren waited for her to say she'd thought he was a girl, but she didn't speak; he supposed she was waiting for the name. He gave her the full name, Opal Avery Garland.

If she's not here, I'll tell you so, but if she's here, all I can tell you is I can't tell you.

So is she there?

Just wait a minute now. I ain't magic.

Loren listened for telling background noises such as the singing of songs, but there was nothing. It seemed pretty much hopeless. Cass and Papaw continued to argue. When they ran out of foods, they started over at the first food. Loren was prepared to slam the phone down if either one of them came into the kitchen. He wanted the woman to hurry back. He wanted to explain that the wrong person had been admitted and he would like to make an exchange.

I don't see that anybody's here, the woman said.

You mean you can't tell me if there is?

I mean there's not as far as I can tell.

But as far as you can't tell, maybe she's there.

I can't tell you she's here, because she's not.

Loren thanked the woman and hung up the phone. She hadn't been any use at all. He ate two rumballs and went back to the living room to wait for a break in the conversation so he could demand to know once and for all what was going on.

Maybe it didn't have to do with food at all, Cass was saying.

What would it have to do with, then?

Maybe she was born that way.

Born that way? Avery?

Yeah, sure, why not?

So no matter what she ate or how I raised her she'd be this way now no matter what kind of food or anything.

Maybe. I mean it's just a idea.

Papaw considered it. Well, he said eventually, I don't care what way you're born, that's no call to go being like Avery is.

I know she's not at that hospital, said Loren.

What do you know that for?

I called them and asked.

They examined him as if he were a monkey that had just learned to speak.

They told me nobody by that name's even there.

Look here, said Papaw. You think it's easy on her living all alone with you when what she needs is a man of the house and all you do is eat? Cause if you ain't the man of the house, what is it exactly you're spose to be?

Papaw's questions never had any answers to them. He had no idea how to ask questions.

Leave him alone, said Cass, we done picked on him enough.

Maybe you done picked at him, but I ain't.

I'm sorry about them peas last night, said Cass.

Whoever died from a pea? said Papaw. You could eat peas all

day and never get fat. Vegetables like peas that's from the earth, your stomach has got to labor at the minerals like if you was a coal miner you ain't got no sack of taters. You'd get some common sense stead of book smart. Avery, she's all wrong in her head, but she's got common sense.

People who distinguished between being book smart and having common sense weren't as smart as they wanted to be, so they tried to make themselves feel better by denying that Loren had common sense on top of being book smart. If anyone had no common sense, it was Cass, because it made no sense that he would apologize for anything, ever, and Loren was suspicious.

She can put things together, Papaw continued, and make things. It didn't come natural to her, course, cause she's a woman, and she tried so hard to be the other way, so every time she has to make things she tries real hard where I just make the things. Like when your tiller broke down Cass and she figgered out they weren't no ull in it.

Cass reddened. That ull was too clean to see it on the dipstick.

A tiller ain't got a dipstick, you dipstick. That's horseshit anyhow.

I'd like to see her shoot a dang turkey.

She's got twiced the common sense you've got, dipstick.

Then she's got three times what you've got, old man.

Then three and two makes five and I've got five morn you got.

The purpose of common sense, Loren thought, was to help Papaw and Cass feel good about themselves. They got sad and depressed and miserable like everyone else, and their belief in common sense was all they had to comfort them during those times.

So then it's common sense, said Cass, to want to be the opposite of what you was born to the world to be.

Avery wasn't born to nothing but what she chose.

She didn't choose to be a woman. It's got nothing to do with sense.

Common sense is to know what ull is.

So where is she, then? said Loren.

They looked surprised he was still around.

There ain't just one hospital in the whole entire world, said Papaw.

There's only one on top of Chilhowee Mountain, though.

Then I guess the mountain's where she is till you stop eating so much.

Loren thought Papaw was a more likely reason for her to leave than he was.

There's some things I ain't talking about, said Papaw. I don't believe in it and I reckon it ain't meant to be and I won't say nothing about it except this what I'm sayin to you right now and that's the last of it that I'll say.

But Papaw didn't seem to Loren like he meant that. Sure he had beliefs about tillers and vegetables and meats, but he didn't have morals, or at least he didn't think anything was wrong, except for eating. Loren kept thinking back to the driveway of Carnetta Sledge. He had a picture in his head of this woman: long raven-black hair, green eyes, turquoise jewelry, and a wrinkled India-print dress. Where he'd gotten the image, he didn't know, and she probably wasn't a real person at all. Loren knew of Mother's girlfriends in the past because Mother had thought he wasn't as smart as he was, and she had spoken on the telephone late at night when a normal child would have been sleeping, but that was long ago. Now her body wasn't right for her, it got more wrong all the time, and there was no use anymore in going out into the world. Loren didn't think it was possible that he'd caused that to be the case. Eating seemed to him like a separate thing, and he tried in his mind not to listen to Papaw, but

Papaw was frowning at him as though he were nothing more than a sack of potatoes. He considered the notion that Papaw and Cass and Ruby were right, and Mother was wrong. Papaw and Cass and Ruby only wanted him be thin, for his own sake, and if he was stuck in this body for the rest of his life, they wanted him to learn to be a man and stop wanting impossible things. They'd all stopped wanting impossible things long ago, if they had ever wanted impossible things at all.

The idea that he might be wrong hovered in his head, upsetting him sporadically for the next hour as he wandered the yard, going to its four corners, each surveyed and marked with stakes that had orange ribbons tied around them. He looked up at the mountain. The hospital had seemed awfully expensive. Probably Mother had other children she'd never told him about, and they lived together on the mountain with a view over Loren's head all the way to Maryville.

Loren made his way into Cass's dark garage, to the back closet, where he hid himself and listened to the outside world. Most of the next two days, the part that wasn't school, passed for him inside this closet. He stored a jar of peanut butter there and ate it sometimes, but mostly he managed to quit before he was full, before his side started hurting. He enjoyed the small space. Maybe they'd buried Mother alive. Or they'd plucked her heart out and sold it for money, or she was just disgusted with him, plain and simple. Through the wall he could hear conversations between Cass and Papaw, Cass and Delia, Cass and Gurney Flinchum, Cass and Ruby. They talked about Riverlake, which came up only when Loren was out of sight. They could talk about it for days. They talked about the merits of various types of guns. Loren had always hated guns; maybe it was time to change his mind. Maybe the world had shifted and Ruby would be his mother now, and Cass his father, and Mother was only glitches in his head, but memories seemed so real—the peanut butter, the country drives.

You should of smacked her face, he heard Delia say through the wall, and in the muddle of Cass's response Loren heard his own name.

Good, he should stay out.

He needs to eat dinner, Ruby said at some point.

He needs to eat dinner like I need a hole in my head.

That was an interesting expression. Loren wondered if Cass had made it up himself. He wished someone were trapped with him in the dark so he could share the silence, someone he could touch, someone like me, but as long as he believed I controlled myself, I controlled myself during the times that I existed, and he was scared of his real thoughts.

Nobody ever did any boy things with him, Ruby said.

I don't act like a girl, whether or not I go fishing.

You never go fishing. You don't know how to fish.

You pull the line out, and there's either fish on it or there ain't.

There's more to it than that, and you don't know what.

That's a crock of shit. Loren don't wanna go anyway.

The survey men are gonna come at ten.

He'll cry when the hooks hurt the fish.

Sounds like you at least know the basics.

What basics? Cass shouted.

That there's a hook, and you hook fish with it.

Loren couldn't tell if it was tomorrow when they meant to take him, but it scared him to know the future before the future had arrived. He didn't want to be scared of going fishing. He should fall into the act and see what came of it, but what if he hooked his own skin and died of lockjaw? He'd stumble into the lake and drown. If he hooked a corpse's body at the bottom of the lake and caused it to surface, would they think he'd killed it? Somewhere another door slammed. He flipped through the pages of his drawing pad, straining to see the words in the dim light. No one had laid eyes on his lists of road names, birds he'd seen, books he'd read, stars in the northern cosmos, countries of the world, the names of Smoky Mountain peaks, every constellation Mother had made up for him. It was important not to fall asleep with his pen uncapped, or the ink would dry up. He dreamt the gravel cut his feet as he crossed the howling dark in which he never stopped sweating, and Mother had just bought those socks. Why wasn't he more grateful? He ate them to make up for it. Cass woke him up at nine with a fishing pole in his hand, and Loren felt a twinge of apprehension as he realized what was happening. He rubbed his eyes and tried to brace himself.

Get up and put your fishing clothes on, said Cass. When I was your age I got to the fishing hole every morning at the crack of dawn.

I thought you didn't fish.

Where'd you hear that? I never said that.

I don't remember, Loren said.

That's cause I never said it.

Which clothes are my fishing clothes?

Clothes you fish in.

I don't have any, though.

Come on, now. Every kid has fishing clothes.

Loren closed his eyes and wished he were still asleep, and he kept them shut even while he got up to change into a clean T-shirt and jeans. He heard dishes clanking in the kitchen and supposed Cass was preparing food to take on the fishing trip. He wished Cass were tied up on a leash somewhere, but Loren couldn't picture it; he could imagine only the opposite, with Cass tying up other people, children, litters of kittens. He entered the kitchen, where Cass stood at the counter spreading peanut butter onto bread.

What kind of sandwiches are you fixing?

Peanut butter.

Peanut butter and what?

Jelly, said Cass without looking up.

Loren didn't see any. What flavor of jelly? he asked.

It'll be a surprise.

I don't like surprises.

Yeah you do. You just ain't never got surprised yet.

Loren wondered why Delia wasn't fixing the food; maybe she was tied up with ropes in the bedroom, and he should set her free, but now she stood in the hall, eyes so sleepy they looked blind, and Loren was glad she existed. She probably knew how to fish; she came from the lake and could show them how. She combed her tangled hair, and when they were ready, Cass loaded poles and a bright red tacklebox and a big bucket into the car.

What's Dusty's truck doing at the road? asked Loren.

It's not doing nothing. It's just sitting there.

Rolls of steel tape lay beside the truck in the tall grass with an old rusty chainwheel. Loren pointed to a metal instrument like a telescope on a tripod and asked, What's that?

Theodolite, said Cass.

It looks like a robot.

Wish we had a dog. Dogs love to fish.

Loren didn't see why a dog would want to fish.

Always took my dog fishing when I was a kid. You should make Avery get you a dog once she gets home from that old hospital.

This was more than Cass had spoken to Loren in his whole life put together. Loren wanted to show some gratefulness by keeping the conversation going, so he asked the dog's name.

They wasn't one particular name.

What's a theodolite do?

They was lots of different names, whichever one was alive.

Loren wondered which question he should complain that Cass wasn't answering.

They were the neighbors' dogs. They followed me.

You didn't have a dog?

Neighbors had enough to go around.

There weren't any neighbors. You grew up on Papaw's farm.

You don't know nothing about it.

There weren't any other houses.

You wasn't even born yet. How do you know what they was?

I'm not trying to say you're lying. Never mind.

If you think I'm a liar, how come you keep asking me questions?

If there'd been other houses, they'd still be here, and they're not.

Guess somebody must have went and tore em down.

Loren thought there'd be evidence in the form of bricks or driveways. It was impossible to eradicate a driveway without leaving some trace. The idea that Cass would admit to lying, though, was unbelievable, so it must be true. Perhaps the houses had been buried beneath Tellico Lake when the Tennessee Valley Authority had closed the dam's gates. Since the lake was Loren's exact same age, it was his closest companion now in the valley. He was terrified to be near it. In a common nightmare Mother was driving him into the lake. Around any bend in this area one could suddenly discover that a road headed straight into water. If driveways could be eradicated, the flooded roads hidden around bends would have disappeared. They'd deteriorated over time, but Loren would be an old man before they were gone, assuming he lived to adulthood. What if the government decided to build another dam? He knew farms had been buried by Tellico Lake, because silos still rose from the water at Carson Island, and all along Calderwood Highway. Although the closest channel of the lake was at least three miles from

Papaw's farm, it seemed Cass's childhood neighbors had been buried beneath it, and their dogs committed to a watery grave. Clearly Cass had a reason not to want to discuss it. This hinted to Loren that Mother too had legitimate reasons not to talk about the past. Everything from before Tellico Dam's construction, Loren was realizing, was too painful to talk about. The whole family had awful secrets buried underwater. They associated Loren with those secrets, since he and the lake had arrived here together.

They got into the truck, Loren sitting between Cass and Delia, and drove toward the highway. Immediately Delia lit a menthol cigarette. When she finished it, she started another one. Loren watched old men churning mowers through their yards, because it was spring, the grass was finally growing, and he was glad he wasn't any of these men. The day was colorless and hazy. The mountain wasn't crisp against the sky. Maybe he was wrong; he wanted to take the men's places, even though they were in their fifties, sixties. That was okay. When he saw the mountain crest, it looked so vague and yellow it was little more than a cloud that held no rain.

Cass pulled into a gas station on 411 near the Monroe County line to buy bait. There's lures in the tacklebox, said Delia, but Cass didn't hear; he was on his way into the service station. Loren followed him inside and blinked his eyes to adjust to the lower light. He curled his nose at the stink of fish. The man working the counter had black tattoos all down the rough skin of his arms.

We need some worms, said Cass.

The man gestured to a long wall of lidded Styrofoam cups and grunted.

What's the difference between the cups?

They're different sizes.

The worms?

The cups.

Cass hurried to the counter with a large cup.

Them's night crawlers, the man said.

Okay, Cass said. Good.

You don't fish much, the man said.

It's just been a while. Everything's a little different nowadays.

They drove another few miles down 411 to the turnoff for Tellico Blockhouse. Loren was praying that they wouldn't drive into the lake. They could crest a hill and find themselves headed straight for the lake. Cass might think it fun to charge his truck into the water. There were men who taught children to swim by throwing them into water over their heads. Loren was thankful Mother didn't care about swimming. It made no difference to Mother whether or not Loren ever swam, which he intended never to do. In fact she wanted him to stay away from water. He felt sure she'd be terribly upset to know Cass was threatening to drive him into the lake. If this road had ever navigated a low valley, Loren would drown. But when they reached the top of a hill, Cass pulled off and parked. For now Loren was safe.

Bet you can't wait to catch your first fish.

Loren managed to grunt a response.

Bet you wonder why your mama never did nothing like this.

Delia smoked two cigarettes during their walk down to the water. An old fort stood across the channel. They crossed the foundation of an old blockhouse from the French and Indian War. They had walked a quarter of a mile, and Loren was out of breath, but Delia just smoked and walked and never seemed to breathe at all. It was possible to measure time and distance by her number of cigarettes. He knew he should be able to walk farther without getting tired. He should be able to skip meals, but he was angry that everyone had forgotten to feed him all morning. He hated that he was hungry, but he couldn't help it.

I didn't have breakfast, he announced.

Nobody did, said Cass. Who the hell eats breakfast?

Mother says breakfast is the most important meal.

Your mama never ate breakfast a day in her life.

Loren could remember the two of them eating Grape Nuts together, but as Cass's words resonated in his head, the memory began to feel like a fabrication. It was easy to take Mother's image and give it food and a spoon and call it real.

Wait till we catch some fish, said Cass.

I don't want to eat fish, said Loren, I want breakfast.

He blushed when Delia giggled at him. Catch one fish and you can have something to eat, Cass said. Just one fish. But he wouldn't be able to catch one and Cass would say go farther into the water, wade toward the open sea where there's fish, and Loren would be swept away. He wished he weren't scared. The other name for rabies was hydrophobia, and he hoped he wasn't coming down with it. His fear of water had remained at about the same level, though, for his whole life.

At the dock Cass picked up a pole and got a hook from the tacklebox. When he tried to tie it to the line, he cut his finger open, and the hook fell out into murky water. He didn't get angry about it. Whatever was happening back at the house at ten o'clock this morning meant Cass had to be nice to Loren for the time being. He got a second hook and managed to tie it on and cast the baitless line into the water. It sank in a lazy droop. Cass tried to reel it back in, but the hook snagged something, and he tugged until it broke.

Maybe it was a fish, said Loren.

It wasn't no fish. You think I'd let a fish get away?

Delia took a red-and-white float from the tacklebox and said, You use one of these.

Loren didn't want it to seem like he and Delia knew more about fishing than Cass did, so he asked Cass what it was.

A float, said Delia.

Nobody asked you to come.

So it floats on top of the water? said Loren.

What else would it do?

Loren hated seeming dumber than he really was, but it was all he could think of to say. His stomach growled while Cass attached a float and a hook onto the second pole. His tying of the float looked wrong, but Loren didn't question it.

Is there a ranger that works here? said Delia. Maybe he'd know how to put the float on.

Loren worried for Delia as Cass kicked the air. Why wasn't she more careful about what she said; did she want to get hurt? She held her hands in the heart-shaped back pockets of her jeans. Get the float on right, Loren repeated to himself, pacing the short length of the pier, do it right do it right, and finally the line was ready. Cass baited it with a night crawler half an inch thick and gave it to Loren, who sat down on the floating end of the dock and cast the line into the water while Cass fixed the second rod.

What kind of fish will we catch? he asked.

I don't have a goddamn clue.

There's carp and bass and walleye and catfish, Delia said.

As if that's all there is, Delia.

Mainly it's just bluegills close to shore.

Loren had always believed he could transport himself into another life if he thought hard enough. He was unable to think that hard. There were distractions. He waited fifteen minutes without a nibble. When he reeled his line in, the worm was gone. Perhaps it had swum away to the Indian graveyards beneath the lake. Seven Cherokee villages were rotting in these waters. Thinking of it made Loren scoot back from the edge of the dock. After another fifteen minutes he brought his line up and again there was no worm.

This isn't fun, he said.

It ain't picked up yet.

He felt faint from going so long without eating. He rebaited the line and sat down with a thump that rocked the dock. Waves lapped at the water's edge, splashing at his bare feet. He wiggled his toes in the polluted water. I think I'd have more fun if I weren't so hungry, he said.

He wondered why Delia wasn't helping him persuade Cass that it was time to eat; surely she was starving. He hadn't seen her eat breakfast.

Okay, Cass said, go on.

Loren opened the bag of sandwiches.

I thought you could manage to catch a fish first, but it don't matter.

He was glad Cass had come to understand. Maybe Cass would stop being so illogical. Loren's main concern was the sandwich. He was careful not to unwrap the aluminum foil too quickly; otherwise his enthusiasm would look to come from being fat and not from genuine hunger. Finally, his sandwich in hand, he bit into it. Right away he could tell something wasn't right. At first he kept chewing; then his gag reflex took notice of whatever terrible thing was congealing in his mouth, and he spat the chewed lump into the water. Cass watched him, grinning. When he unpeeled the two sticky slices of bread from each other, lardy mayonnaise shone alongside the peanut butter; each was spotted with the other.

That's why I couldn't remember the jelly, said Cass, it wasn't jelly at all.

Cass unwrapped his own sandwich and chewed it with his mouth wide open, and Loren turned away and tried not to gag again.

That's disgusting, said Loren.

I'm disgusting?

The sandwich.

Don't blame me; blame Delia.

I saw you fix it, Loren said.

Delia, tell him.

I fixed the sandwich, she said softly, as Loren pitched the rest of his soggy bread into the lake. He had begun to think of Delia as an ally. That would have to change.

We could have used your bread for bait, said Cass.

Fish wouldn't eat it either.

I'm eating it, ain't I? Cass baited his hook with the gluey bread of his own sandwich and cast the line and said, Watch me, you ain't right on everything there is.

Maybe Mother had known exactly what would happen. He watched carefully in case this was what she wanted him to learn. He looked around for trees she could have been hiding behind. He opened his mouth, but before he could speak, Cass said, Hush or you'll scare the fish, so the three of them stared silently at the red float. A motorboat drifted across an inlet of the lake, and Loren tried to estimate how many miles it was across the water. He wondered if the water by the dock was even deep enough for fish to swim in.

It all mixes up inside you, said Cass. Peanut butter, mayonnaise, all of it.

Not at the same time, it doesn't.

That's what I'm trying to tell you, boy.

Cass didn't have any idea what he was saying. Mother was the only one who thought about the words she spoke, and that was why she pronounced them correctly and why she had disappeared. It was just too much of a burden. Loren looked at his watch, never thinking this action would make Cass ask him, Don't you like to spend time with me?

I like spending time with you.

No, you don't. You hate every minute of it.

When Cass's line jumped, he lost his rod to the rocky water of the shore. He jumped into the lake. The water came up to his waist. Loren hoped he'd slip on algae and drown. There'd have to be another funeral. Cass swept the rod up into his hands and reeled it in. The blades of his shoulders seemed to grapple with all the water of Tellico Lake at once, and he won this battle: he'd hooked the left eye of a fish that thrashed in the air as Loren looked away, wincing.

Bull's-eye, said Cass.

That's bluegill, said Delia.

Get the hook out, said Loren. It's in pain.

Fish don't get pain. Get it out yourself if you're in such a hurry.

Loren cringed as the scaly body swung into his chest. It looked up into Loren's eyes without blinking, but Loren felt like his eyes were being clamped shut, so he couldn't even try to pull the hook out as the fish shook so violently.

Hurry up, Cass said, mocking him. It's in pain. Delia giggled.

You can't just tear its eye out, Loren said.

Should have thought of that before you came fishing.

Loren lowered the contorting fish slowly into the bucket, which Cass had filled with algae-colored water. Loren hoped the water soothed the pain he knew the fish felt. It swam in pan-icked lines from side to side as Delia reached down and pulled the hook out.

Can't we throw it back in? Loren asked.

Sure, throw it back in if you want, Cass said, but when Loren reached for the bucket, Cass smacked his hand away and said, Jinx. It seemed that the fish would die. Cass proceeded to catch four more, but Loren didn't catch any, and Delia just smoked. The fish touched each other in the bucket as they swam. Loren didn't feel hungry anymore. Looking at the bucket reminded him that he hadn't eaten all day, but he didn't want to eat the fish or even think about fish. Eventually Delia ran out of cigarettes and it was time to leave. But we can't leave till we go swimming, said Cass. That's half of what we came here for, was so Loren could go swimming.

Loren's heart stopped: this was exactly what he'd feared. He'd sensed the threat all along. He needed never to stop trusting his intuition.

I need some cigarettes, said Delia. I ain't got no more.

Loren needs him some swimming time, don't you, Loren?

I don't really like swimming that much.

I guess that's because you don't know how to swim?

He turned red. Of course I know how.

Let's see you try then.

I don't have bathing trunks. These are my fishing clothes.

We'll take off our shirts. Don't matter if we get our shorts wet.

Loren could see that people didn't change. If at any moment he didn't trust them, he should keep distrusting them his whole life. That was how to protect himself. It was what animals did in the forest, and from this day forward he'd do it too. For now, it was too late, unless Cass wasn't serious. Cass had spoken earlier of being a liar. He was sad that his mother had died. He felt apprehensive about his land being sold. Loren could tell what a theodolite was. The very sound of the word meant it was a way of taking the land away.

Some folks teaches kids to swim just throwing em in the water.

If you do that, Loren wanted to say, Mother will kill you. What Cass wanted Loren to say, he thought, was that he himself would kill Cass. He'd curl his hands into fists and fight to the death. The winner could stay out of the water. Cass didn't care whether or not Loren knew how to swim. To suggest a fight, though, would be a bluff, because Loren didn't know how to fight; for that matter, he didn't know how to bluff.

Maybe I could leave yuns here to swim, said Delia, and go buy cigarettes.

Delia didn't understand that men were volatile and could turn on women for no reason at all. It was important to be careful. Delia didn't know that. She was making everything worse. Loren braced himself. Either he was about to be thrown into water, or Delia was about to be struck. He'd never seen Cass hit a girl, but he knew Cass could do it. Mother had warned him about men. They were dangerous in many ways, all of which she'd described; also she'd explained how not to get in fights. The world was treacherous. The greatest peril of all was water. In the dream of Mother's that recurred most, she took Loren to visit the dam, and they walked onto the lock gates. Only a metal railing separated them from certain death a hundred feet below. Mother heard a sound behind her, and turned. A white bird was flying toward her, in the path of the sun. Look at this beautiful bird, Loren. But when she turned back around, he'd fallen into the lock. My baby, she cried, but no one could hear. The first thing she did was to die inside, forever; the second was to jump, a hundred feet down. Falling, falling forever, hitting water. Sinking into the water. She fought her way up through the water. Her son's body lay motionless on the surface. She swam desperately toward it, but she couldn't get closer. Although it was daytime, bright stars shone in the sky. It was too dark for her to see if Loren was still breathing. A terrible noise. The lock gates were opening. Water began rushing out. She tried to scream, but produced no noise; all she could hear were the grinding gates as Loren was carried away into the Tennessee River. And when she woke from these nightmares, she came to Loren in the night and woke him too, held him close and promised she'd never let go of his hand; and it made Loren upset, having just woken from dreams himself, faced by all the emptiness his mother could muster. Something was wrong with what she was saying.

He grew older, remembering what she had promised, thinking everything would be alright, swearing he'd save her from the fate of her dreams by never going anywhere near lakes. Now that there was nothing to protect her from, he'd drown. He braced himself. The earth was quiet. He stood in the eye of a great storm. Any minute now it would pass. He heard Cass laughing. He opened his eyes.

What in tarnation are you holding yourself that way for?

Loren unclenched his fists and tried to relax his shoulders. Delia was watching too. He wondered how much time had passed.

You think I'd really throw you into the lake?

You said that was what you'd do.

I said that's how some people teach their kids to swim. Wish to God your Papaw'd taught us that way, then we'd know how.

You don't know how to swim?

Course I don't know. How would I know how to swim? This lake ain't been here forever. You think everything's always been just the same as now, just cause you weren't born. Guess we'd better go and get this woman her cigarettes.

Loren carried the bag of uneaten peanut-butter-and-mayonnaise sandwiches uphill to the car, Delia carried the fishing rods and tacklebox, and Cass carried the bucket of fish. Any strangers they encountered would think Loren was Cass and Delia's son. He'd blurt out an explanation, but he didn't have any proof to offer. Thank God no one passed them on their way to the truck. He could pretend that this day hadn't existed. It was possible that people would spot him on the highway. He would hunch down below the dashboard. If Cass asked why, he wouldn't explain; after all, no one else in the family explained things, and if he didn't either, he might start to fit in. But when Loren saw how hard it was to identify the faces of drivers speeding down 411, he decided not to bother hunching down. No one knew him. He led an isolated existence. There were the teachers at school, the Primitive Baptists from the church. He barely remembered—his memory didn't waste time on the faces of strangers—so he looked fearlessly out the window at cars headed south toward Atlanta. Two shacks at the county line promised *FIREWORKS* on signs bigger than the structures themselves. The marquee of the Trigonia Missionary Baptist Church said *Read about the living waters.* There were too many different types of Baptists for Loren to keep track of. He kept his observations to himself; the drive consisted only of silence and the occasional curse. Cass had talked himself out while fishing. That was okay. Even back at home Cass didn't speak until the phone rang and he had to discuss driveway connections. Delia spent the afternoon on the couch watching talk shows on TV. During a commercial break she turned to Loren and said, You're boring.

Loren shrugged. Eventually Delia curled up and fell asleep, and Loren crept away; he didn't like her anymore. Her face never looked like it was thinking about things. Suddenly Loren felt a powerful desire to see Mother. If this were a few days ago, he'd have gone straight to the kitchen and demanded to see her, but he had come to understand that he was more powerful when he kept thoughts to himself instead of speaking them. He looked down at the carpet for a long time, trying to think what to do next, but it didn't work, because he was thinking about thinking. He couldn't think when he was aware he was thinking. Maybe he was actually thinking things only when he was thinking about thinking them, and the other times were dreams.

Delia woke up and walked into the kitchen. You're gonna have to cut them fish heads off yourself if you want it cooked, Loren heard her saying, and Cass snorted. Loren still had his jar of extra-crunchy peanut butter stored in the garage, and he went to eat some of it, but he quit before he was full. His left side didn't hurt yet. He put the jar away. He walked out to the front corner of the yard, which was marked with an orange ribbon wrapped around a metal stake. He found all five fish floating on their sides in the bucket. He could smell their scales mingling with the scent of trees and the stale water. He looked at the mountain's rampart and considered his phone call and made plans to investigate. He tried to remember if he'd ever woken from dreams that had seemed to last for weeks. There was still a chance this was one.

He went back to his closet in the rear of the garage. He climbed across a wicker chest to the corner where he'd built a wall of objects between himself and the light shining through the crack under the door. I wish you'd gone ahead and done it, Cass said through the wall. I wish you'd just go get yourself some once and for all.

Loren dreamt that Delia moved out, and then she did. She told Cass he was twenty years too old for her, which Loren supposed was true, and she accused him of being hairy and disgusting and stupid and ignart and dared him to hit her. Loren listened for the sound of hitting or of falling but heard neither. She dared him again and again. She seemed genuinely to want it to happen, but a truck pulled into the drive; when Loren opened the closet door and peeked out through cracks in the paint that covered the garage window, he saw that it was Gurney. Delia had called Gurney, Gurney was her new man, and if Cass didn't want to hit her why didn't he just hit Gurney. That was exactly what Cass did. She won't never get no money now, he yelled at Gurney, punching his face. You think you can't arm wrestle my sister well get a load a me.

Gurney punched Cass back. It was lucky Loren had found this place in the garage. Delia got in the passenger seat of Gurney's S-10. Blood from Gurney's nose dripped into his mouth when he opened his mouth to say, That diesel dyke sister of yours is strongern you. He got in the truck and sped down the driveway and away. Cass waved his fist at them. Delia Sledge, I hope you crust up and die. Stay on welfare the rest of your life, you welfare slut.

Sledge, thought Loren. His heart skipped a beat. He'd never known her last name. The truck sped down the road. Loren opened the garage door, but by then Cass had stomped across the mud patch, holding his bleeding nose, around the house and out of sight. Loren wanted to follow, but he was scared. Cass might get caught up in his adrenaline and hit Loren too. Better to go in the house for a while and wait. It wasn't often that he got a whole house to himself. Cass had stocked the icebox with popsicles. Loren didn't even like popsicles, but he ate one; then it occurred to him to save the intake of calories for food he actually enjoyed. He sat on the back porch in the breeze, his eyes settling on the shed at the border of Cass's property and Papaw's woods. That was probably where Cass was. It had been about three minutes, which was enough time to calm Cass down. Loren decided, as he walked toward it, that he would skip supper. He'd grow thinner that way.

As he made his way to the shed, he phrased the question in his head that he'd ask about Delia. Does Delia have a sister? I think I know someone at school named Sledge. Do you know anyone else named Sledge? Mysteries could uncover themselves when he least expected it. He pulled the latch and swung the shed door open. In the dark Cass was hunched in a chair, his Wranglers at his legs. He spoke to his crotch in a thick rush of a voice, shaking his arms. I swear I'll do it. This'll fix you up real good, you bitch.

Loren turned to run, but Cass was too fast. In a blur of movement, Cass was holding his legs, and Loren was upside down. Cass spun him right-side up, and Loren smelled aftershave. Cass's eyes were laughing at him, the dark dimples too, their curves red like raw ground chuck. Cass laughed in slow motion. His fly was still open.

Scared of it. Ain't ya.

When he let go, Loren wanted to be watching himself dropping so he would know how to land. He thought of telling Cass he was sorry about Delia, but he didn't feel bad for Cass, so he was silent. Cass went back into the shed, and Loren sat on the back stoop of the house until cold drizzle began misting the yard. The mountain was invisible to him. Then the clouds burst open with driving rain that plastered his clothes to his skin. The cotton clung to him, working its way into his folds until he felt too naked to remain outdoors. He jumped when he saw Ruby in the kitchen below the pots of violets drooping from the dusty sill. She was heating water for iced tea.

Have you seen Cass? He's spose to be at my house. It's the full of the moon, and I don't want that poor soul getting into any more trouble.

He's not a poor soul, said Loren. He's not nice. Anyway the full moon's not for days.

She ran her finger along the spine of a violet leaf.

It wasn't even a half moon on Easter.

I spect you don't drink tea.

I don't want to live with him anymore.

Get on now, she said. I need some time to my own.

Why are you here? Have you talked to my mother?

Wherever Avery is, when she gets back, she's gonna be a lot happier.

Happier than what? She's already happy. She's always been happy.

You have a limited perspective, Lorn. I grew up with her. I knew her when she was your age and I think I know about happiness.

If she's up there on the mountain, why can't I visit her?

If she wanted you visiting her, she never would have gone up there to begin with.

Do you know about Delia's family?

Trash like that probly don't have a family at all.

Did you grow up with her or anything?

Lorn, she's closer to your age than she is mine.

I was wondering if she had a sister.

Why, you lookin to court some trash too?

He couldn't quite explain what he wanted to know. Ruby stirred the water harder, which seemed pointless to Loren. He hoped she hadn't noticed his wet clothes. She never really looked at him anyway, so she probably hadn't. It felt good to peel the cotton from his skin. Sweat beaded on him, which meant he was losing weight. His boils were still there. He didn't like to think about them much. Dreams changed him, every night. It wasn't safe how they seeped so freely into the past. He tried to look at the mountain out the window, but it was still hidden behind fog. It was sinking into the earth with the old leaves. Rocks crept across the land like ivy. In his dream he pissed on them with cold antivenin so he wouldn't get a rash. He could do whatever the hell he wanted.

At school the next morning the guidance counselor brought a new boy to the class, his forehead as flat as a river rock, and Loren thought of the Neanderthals in his textbook. Even Loren could make fun of this person who had different textbooks than everyone else.

You *did* fractions, Miss Rathbone was saying. How can yuns forget ever single thing I stand up here and learn you? Meanwhile Calvin turned the pages of his science fiction book quickly, four or five a minute, with mathematical precision.

How do you think it makes me feel that yuns ignore ever thing I say?

Loren tried to determine whether Calvin was actually reading words.

Lorn, she said, were you listening to me just now?

Some boys laughed. Yes, ma'am, Loren said.

What did I just say?

Were you listening to me just now?

I'm the one ast you, not you me, now *say*.

That's what you said, though. And then you said, What did I
just say?

Saying this didn't make Loren nervous, because he wasn't
doing anything he felt was wrong. If he made fun of Miss Rathbone, she deserved it. She never asked questions she didn't
know the answers to. She'd spent the entire school year asking
one question after another that she already knew the answer to,
or thought she did, and it was a waste of Loren's time to try to
guess which particular answer she wanted at which moment.

Why don't you ask Calvin instead? He looks like he was listening.

Lorn Garland, said Miss Rathbone, I'm surprised at you.

He shrugged and saw that everyone was suppressing laughter. Miss Rathbone kept fussing at him, inches from his face, but
he didn't care as much as he would have before. He wanted to
fail the social studies test on purpose, but he wasn't brave enough
yet to do such a thing. The rest of the day he tried to think of
new ways to make fun of Calvin. He'd be nice to Calvin when
they were alone, he decided, and he'd make fun of Calvin while
they were around Eli and Leland and the rest, but Calvin stayed
in the classroom at recess. Thus Loren's opportunity to become
friends with Eli and Leland was lost. Instead he swung on the
swings watching Chilhowee Mountain until recess was over and
they were back in the hot classroom where Miss Rathbone
talked about biomes for the entire afternoon. I'm gonna keep

learnin yuns biomes until yuns has got biomes right, she said, and it don't matter if that's today or tomorrow or forever. I'll fail ever last one of you. Yuns had the whole playground to blab your mouths on and I said be quite.

When Eli belched, the class burst into laughter. Miss Rathbone went for her paddle drawer, but the intercom beeped before she could get it out. It was another bomb threat, and the principal said evacuate the building.

Yuns better not say a word while you're out there, Miss Rathbone yelled. When she went to talk to the other teachers, the boys all fell out of line and talked about NASCAR and how they wished it was still the Civil War. Eli kicked dust at Leland, who kicked dust at the other Leland, who kicked it back at Leland, and then Miss Rathbone was right behind Eli, stooping to lift him by the armpits. He grinned when she spun him around.

I didn't know you liked me that way, he said.

What was you just sayin there a minute ago?

Oh, I was just saying you can sure tell you're drunk when you go to take a piss and the piss talks back to you when it hits the water.

Come down here from Knoxville think you can be this way, you little turd, well I am not gonna let you do it to me.

What makes you think I'd wanna do it to you in the first place?

Miss Rathbone took a handful of Eli's hair and tried to drag him away, but he Indian-burned her wrist and darted between her legs toward the monkey pines.

I'm gonna get you expelled! she cried out. She threw her high-heel shoe at him, but it missed by more than twenty feet. She rushed off to call for Mr. Ownby.

Don't go in the school, Eli yelled to her, it might blow up.

I wish you'd blow your own self up, she yelled back.

Loren didn't want anyone to die, but he did hope the school

would blow up. Mother would hear about it and return home. Also he wouldn't have to go back to school.

This is fun, said Eli. We should get someone to call in a bomb threat every day. They have to evacuate every time.

You seem to know all about it, said Lyhugh.

Eli laughed. You know what's funny? She's in there saying, Mr. Ownby, Mr. Ownby, you've gotta expel Eli, and Mr. Ownby's just saying shove it, bitch, I'm trying to find a bomb.

Eli picked a dandelion and ate it, stem first. It's good for you to eat flowers, he said, rubbing his stomach. It makes you smell good.

Miss Rathbone followed Mr. Ownby out of the school past the portable classrooms. Mr. Ownby pushed Eli up against a walnut tree. You're in a lot of trouble, he threatened.

She tried to pull my hair out. See where some of it's pulled out?

There's no more bomb, Mr. Ownby told the class. Get back inside the room.

He seemed to look specifically at Loren. Loren figured that was because of his weight, but most people looked away from him instead of toward him. Maybe Mr. Ownby saw that Loren was an orphan now and needed help. There was supposed to be a support network of teachers and principals and others who cared about orphaned children.

Everybody saw her pull my hair out, said Eli.

Mr. Ownby turned tiredly to the class. Did you see Miss Rathbone pull his hair out?

There's some of it right yonder in the grass by that dead bird, said Leland.

Okay, said Mr. Ownby. Go inside. That's all I needed to know.

Loren hoped Miss Rathbone might be fired right there on the spot, but Mr. Ownby only trudged off to his office and left everyone in her care. Obviously his attempt to make eye contact hadn't meant he cared anything for Loren. Loren didn't like anyone in the entire county. Even in the surrounding counties and across the mountains in North Carolina, he hated everyone. That was how confident he felt that Mother was far, far away.

It was exciting not to be embarrassed when he failed the pop quiz like everybody else. They hadn't answered in complete sentences, so they all got zeroes. Calvin didn't answer any way at all, and he didn't get a grade. Loren supposed Calvin was too stupid to get a grade. He wouldn't understand what the number meant. Miss Rathbone said to copy every word she read from the textbook. Saturn was the only planet with rings, and she pointed to a picture and said it had five moons and they had best write down five moons or they was more zeroes where those first ones come from, and Loren raised his hand.

What do you want? she screeched. What did I say about no bathroom?

That's not true about the moons. Voyager Two just found some more.

Go to the office. Says it right here in the book. I had it up to here with you.

What do you want me to tell them at the office, that you were wrong?

I don't care what you tell. Just get out of my sight.

Loren wanted to say something else back to her, but he was afraid she'd paddle him. He'd wait to be paddled until he was thin, he decided, because the other kids would be watching from their desks when it happened. That was one thing about Mother's leaving: now he could get in trouble all he wanted, and he never had to be ashamed. They couldn't call her to tell her what he'd done, because she barely even existed, and they'd learn their lesson if they tried calling Cass or Ruby or Papaw. He ran his finger along the bricks on his way to the principal's office, where he waited by the secretary's desk counting stars on the American flag. When Mr. Ownby was ready, and Loren was inside, Mr. Ownby said, You know what Miss Rathbone just told me on that speaker? Thirty-five years of teaching, and nobody's upset her like you just did.

You've got me confused with Eli.

If she said it's true, it's true, said Mr. Ownby.

Eli was the one she meant.

How would I confuse Eli with you?

Loren looked down at himself and shrugged.

I don't mean because of what you look like. I know who you are.

Loren's heart started to pound. Mr. Ownby's paddle had three holes to make it hurt worse.

Open up your eyes, said Mr. Ownby. I'm just playing. She didn't tell me anything. I don't like that nasty old woman any more than you do. Don't worry about it.

I don't want to go back to class, Loren said.

Mr. Ownby nodded. How's that mama of yours?

How did you know about her?

You exist, don't you?

Loren looked down at himself again.

I reckon everybody that's here's got a mama.

That's not what you meant, though.

I grew up around here too. Right over on Montvale Road.

I never heard her say anything about you.

Loren's throat closed up again when Mr. Ownby reached for the drawer. He got the paddle out and held it out for Loren to see. Sure enough there were three holes in it.

I named my paddle after her. See right there.

Loren had no idea what to think about that.

What do you think about that, huh?

Why would you name a paddle after my mother?

To show respect. She was a good friend of mine.

Does she know you named it after her?

Don't get that way. She don't know about it. We had what you might call a falling out. I did some stuff to upset her. I can't go into it. I'm the principal of the school.

Then why did you think I was Eli if you knew exactly who I was?

You're a funny little kid. Get on back to class now. If Miss Rathbone asks what I done to you, you can tell her I beat the crap out of you. Only if you want to, though.

Loren wondered if this was just a game Miss Rathbone and Mr. Ownby played with each other. He didn't like the thought of Miss Rathbone's having the upper hand. He felt pretty sure, though, that against Miss Rathbone, of all people, he could maintain the upper hand. Back in class he suffered through English, during which he could have corrected Miss Rathbone eight times, and then Ruby picked him and Eli both up in her brand-new black Mercury Cougar, because Loren would be staying with her now to help give him a better feeling of community, and Loren nodded, because it was no surprise to him; he'd already made it happen with his mind.

Your stuff it's already at my house, there wasn't much.

She found all your pornos, Eli said.

Have you talked to Mother? said Loren.

I'm sure she's doing better.

Better than what?

Just better than in general. That's what happens, if you ask me. Everything pretty much gets better. Memories, those are nice, but I'd rather look to the future.

That's a big pile of donkey shit, said Eli.

Like living with me will be better than living with Cass, since Cass's house has already happened and mine is where you're fixin to go to.

At least Cass knows how to hunt and fish, said Eli, but you don't know shit.

Cass is not invested in Tradition, said Ruby.

Is Mother invested in tradition?

Well, each of us is his or her own self. I cain't see what you think, and you cain't see what I think, so there cain't neither one of us see what Avery thinks. Which is not that I think it's right for us to think that way but I have been blessed and I do not know what thoughts I'd think in a head like Avery's, the poor thing.

So that means you don't know if she's invested or not?

You realize she was not nice to your Mamaw, which was wrong of her, and often I was moved to feel that as I nursed our mother back to health, my sister Avery was a demon on her other poor sick shoulder nursing her to an early grave because this is the Eighties, when a woman is spose to reach her twilight years.

They drove on Sixmile Road for about three miles and then turned onto Fourmile Road along Sixmile Creek for a couple of miles.

This thing she wants, continued Ruby, of which I will not speak of, will shorten her life. That should be a matter of some concern to you, Lorn. There is somewhat of a unequalness about life spans and you ought to do everything in your power to preserve your way of life. Do you remember when the Cherokees tried to keep us from having electricity wired to our own homes? How many times have we all gone boating out on Tellico Lake?

Loren had never been on either of Dusty's boats on Tellico or any of the other lakes. Apparently Dusty hadn't offered them to Cass for the fishing trip, and if he had, Loren would have refused to set foot on them.

Eli put his headphones on so he wouldn't have to hear Ruby

explain the lake. It was before you were born, Lorn, so of course you've no way to know what I'm fixin to tell you, but in an attempt to prevent our engineers from building that dam, the Cherokees did everything in their power, which lucky for us is not much power at all. The point is I'm surprised at you for taking what comes and being so passive. Would you want to still be using the privy every time you had to pass water? The point is maybe Avery says she wants to do something when really she doesn't want to at all because what she wants and what she does are often divided by a little bit of confusion.

Loren looked around for something to fiddle with to pass the time and eventually settled on the seat belt. He often thought of biting on his fingernails for that same purpose, but he was afraid it would hurt too much and had never tried.

If you ask me, she ought to eat more radishes to get minerals and the sort of energy of the earth, not that I believe any of that witchery, which that's mostly what that is. I think that's hogwash mostly about the vegetables but clearly there's some kind of unbalance in Avery's body perhaps up in the brain where your mind is.

She knows that. That's what she's taking the hormones for.

Often I dream that I am able to take out some of my extra female hormones, said Ruby with a dreamlike and ambitious gaze toward the face of Chilhowee Mountain, and give them to Avery so she'll have enough to get her unbalance cured. We're sisters she and I so I feel our hormones is compatible with each other as a kidney would be or blood.

Loren felt glad that Ruby was so clearly on Mother's side, because he'd had his doubts about her loyalties up until this moment.

That would bandage my relationship with Avery, and perhaps she'd begin attending my quilting group again on the Wednesday nights and playing bridge.

Loren could tell Ruby's house would be a huge improvement over Cass's. Aside from Mother, Ruby was his favorite family member; plus she was a woman, so she automatically understood him better than any man did.

The Cougar wound through the twisty flat places beside the creek until they had reached his new home. It's such a wonderful coincidence that you two's the same age as yourselves, Ruby was telling Loren as he removed himself from the car, cause of course we'd no way of knowing Eli would be part of the family back when you were born.

It smelled like pot roast inside. She'd been cooking for her bridge club, she explained. Eli poked at the casserole. Looks nasty, he said. My mom don't cook shit like that for company.

Your mother does not have company, Ruby said, pouring flour into a bowl.

What would you do if I knocked the casserole on the floor?

I'd give you a good whipping, and then I'd tell Dusty.

What would you really do, though? What if I punched you?

Are you shown off for Lorn? Go outside. I'll tell it to Dusty.

We're gonna play video games. There's no electricity outside.

You don't pay the mortgage. Do what I say or I really will tell Dusty.

You paid the house off in cash, and it's too hot outside.

That's too goddamn bad, cause that's where you're going.

Ruby pushed Eli out the door and slammed it shut. When she saw Loren standing uneasily behind her, she opened it again and ushered him onto the deck too, touching his shoulders carefully as if he was contagious. When he heard the door latched shut behind him, Eli was halfway up the yard, headed for the woods. Loren had to decide immediately whether to run and catch up. The temperature was at least eighty. He imagined himself sweating. He thought of the ladies in Ruby's bridge club, and then the old women at the funeral, gaping at him like he was a talking baboon. Wait up, he called, jogging down the stairs. Eli didn't stop, but he slowed down enough that Loren caught him at the division between the grass and the trees.

I hate that bitch, Eli said.

You mean Ruby?

Who do you think?

I don't know. Ruby, I guess.

I guess you don't think she's a bitch?

I'd just be scared to say it about her.

I'll do it for you. She's a big old bitch.

Loren looked down at his shoes.

Bitch bitch bitch bitch bitch.

How far are we walking?

You scared to say it?

Loren shook his head. I just don't want to.

Look at all that stupid makeup she wears.

He nodded; it was true she wore too much makeup.

Go on and call her a bitch.

She's not all that bad. She's just trying to be nice.

You've got the dumbest family I've ever seen.

I doubt yours is all that smart.

I didn't say they was, but yours takes the cake.

Loren could report to Mother that he and Eli were friends, and she'd be happy for him. He had to be careful not to ruin it. It embarrassed him to break twigs with his steps; it would remind Eli of his weight. He watched his feet rather than the dogwood blossoms that shone amidst the forest's glow. Tent caterpillar nests grew in the cherry trees, waiting to devour the unborn leaves. Eli stomped suddenly on a beetle. I got you good, he said.

I don't understand, said Loren.

Eli took a handful of dirt and threw it at Loren's arms and shirt.

Why'd you do that?

To explain it.

As they went downhill, Loren felt his hair for ticks. Ticks carried Rocky Mountain spotted fever here, although these mountains were the Smokies.

I've got your whole family figured out, said Eli. Your Papaw killed your Mamaw to get rid of your mama. Just look at that nose of his. That's why Cass hates you so much: you're to blame too if your mama is.

Mamaw had died of kidney failure and double pneumonia, and Cass didn't hate Loren, and Mother hadn't cared for Mamaw anyway.

What about Ruby? he asked.

She don't count; she's a woman.

You counted Mother.

Try and explain your own family then.

Eli stopped at a tent caterpillar nest in a wild cherry tree, raised a stick like a sword, and swung it at leaves and air. A glint was in his eye; then he was breaking through the triangle of the nest. Loren couldn't see the worms swarm individually, but he saw the rough brain their bodies made, and Eli jabbed his stick into the nest of babies.

There's a million of the things in there.

Maybe a thousand, said Loren.

Why don't I just poke it open and count.

Eli tore away the outer cuticle of webbing. Strands trailed into the breeze, making the larvae writhe for their lives. They hadn't finished growing. Eli took the ball of bodies in his hand. Loren moved closer and saw at least two hundred squirming caterpillars still clinging to one another and to remnants of the nest. Could they breathe, or had their lungs not formed yet? They burrowed blindly into gluey pigment, nursing at one another's eyes and stripes as Eli squashed them into pulp. Loren couldn't take his eyes off Eli's face. He told himself again that he just wanted his own face to look like Eli's. That was all. Eli put his finger to his tongue to taste the juice, and he tried to count them, but they fell when he pushed Loren playfully against the tree.

I guess I'll just take your word it was a thousand. Except for I ate one, so it's 999.

The trail had vanished into nothing, but they kept walking, pinning back thorns and saplings, and Loren was glad he was getting himself in shape. Soon he would run away to find Mother. First he'd look for her on the mountain top. If she wasn't there, he'd look at the places farthest from water. It was a puzzle he could solve. There were only so many places she could be. She wanted to be found. That was the only reason people went into hiding. If she wasn't expecting someone to find her, she wasn't hiding at all, which wasn't the case, because it was clear to Loren that she was hiding.

But he wanted to pay attention in these moments. Things were subtle with Eli. He said and did things that were difficult to figure out, and Loren needed to stay focused, so he could learn. He followed Eli over a ridge, down the other side, and along the dry bed of Burnt Creek. Soon they reached a cowpond choked with algae and bridged halfway across by a fallen tree. Because he needed to prove his fearlessness to Eli, Loren walked the length of its trunk and back; when he briefly lost his balance, he clenched his eyes shut. He would tumble into the water. Eli would refuse to save him. All Mother's fears were about to come true. Then he realized he wasn't falling, and when he reopened his eyes Eli was uncorking a glass bottle that had been hidden beneath a log. The liquid looked like bloody vinegar, and it woke Loren's eyes up when he smelled it. Dirt had wasted the label away. Eli put the bottle to his lips and swallowed.

That does hit the spot.

What is that?

Try a drink of it.

No thanks.

Go on. You want to.

Loren looked down at his feet and adjusted his shirt to hide where his nipples were poking against it. In the sweaty heat, with dragonflies buzzing from pussywillow to pussywillow, he saw that he was meant to die today at this pond. Everything in his life had been leading up to it. Papaw would have to buy his coffin in the husky section.

If you try it, I won't make fun of you at school anymore.

Mother had always appeared out of nowhere when he began doing anything wrong. She'd stopped him just in time and never even had to yell. He just wasn't that kind of boy.

Honest, Eli said, drinking again. Scout's honor.

You're not a Boy Scout.

Swear to God, then. Can I at least swear to God?

What does it taste like?

Pussies like you always hate it.

You weren't gonna make fun of me anymore.

You ain't drank it yet.

The label didn't say how many calories the stuff had. It couldn't be any more fattening than Kool-Aid. He hadn't eaten all day. He poured a mouthful into himself, and his throat went numb. He prayed to be able to breathe. Eli laughed as Loren's eyes filled with water. He grabbed the bottle and gulped from it and said, Here, your turn again.

Wait a minute, Loren said. His voice felt funny.

There's no wait a minute, you pussy.

It was sinking straight into the chambers of his heart. His scalp itched and his sinuses burned, and he knew he'd go into anaphylactic shock, but he kept on until Eli seized the bottle back.

Goddamn, he said.

Loren shook his head and rubbed his watery eyes. Hot little waves lapped up at his feet. He moved his hips slowly back and forth to rock the log on which they sat.

My mama's fat too, said Eli.

They stared at the pond together.

I'm not making fun. I'm just saying.

Loren looked into Eli's eyes and decided to trust him, at least for now.

Why don't you live with her?

She lives in a trailer.

So what? She's your mother.

I don't guess I have much say in it.

How much of this are you supposed to drink?

You just drink it till you're drunk. It don't matter.

Usually Loren tried not to smile, because it made his face look fatter, but at this moment he couldn't stop grinning. It felt good to sweat. He peeled the label from the bottle.

It's called a fifth.

A fifth of what?

Wine, said Eli, and Loren laughed.

What are you laughing at?

Hell if I know.

This was the first time he had ever cursed in his life. Hell was only half a curse word, but he was proud of it nonetheless.

I hate it here, said Eli.

For a moment Loren was nervous; he thought Eli meant the pond, being with Loren, right now, but he meant the whole county. There was a million things to do in Knoxville, Eli said.

What kinds of things?

Go to the arcade. Go to the mall.

Oh, said Loren, taking another drink.

Eli gestured at the treetops and said, Look at this shit.

It's not so bad, said Loren. He observed the thorns and weeds and bent trunks that stretched up through warty vines. He could feel the wine in his stomach.

At least it won't be here long, said Eli.

What won't?

The woods. The pond.

Ponds don't move.

They do if you build houses on top of them.

Papaw's not building any houses.

That's why we moved here.

You moved here because of Ruby.

Eli shrugged and drank again. I guess so.

Your dad can't develop it. It's not his.

Mostly he does what he wants.

Papaw's had it his whole life.

I guess that's why he's selling it. What a shitty life.

Loren picked up a flat stone and skimmed it across the water in three jumps. He hadn't expected to be able to.

They're all gonna make a bunch of money, said Eli.

Eli tried to skip a stone too, but it sank. Loren wondered why he even cared about the woods; he hadn't walked in them much until this spring.

Some of it's Mother's. She's not selling hers.

Dad tells me this shit cause he figures I never talk to you, since you're fat.

Eli paused to take a drink, then added, I'm just saying. He says a lot of shit about your mama.

Mother told me she'll beat Dusty up if he doesn't watch out.

I hope he don't watch out then, cause I hate his guts.

Do you always hate his guts, or are you just saying that?

I'll hate his guts till I can move out of this retarded place.

Do you hate Ruby's guts too?

I don't guess so. She bought me that Nintendo.

What does Dusty say about my mother?

None of it makes much sense, so I'd say it's bullshit.

Loren thought that probably meant it wasn't bullshit at all.

He said she's fixin herself up for the circus. That's what she wanted all the land money for, was fixin herself up. I don't see why it costs money to join a circus, though. I don't think there even is one anymore. That's just the old days.

Loren was scared of the truth for a number of reasons. Mother had been ashamed of admitting it to him, so it would be highly upsetting. She probably knew in advance its capacity to upset him, because of her wisdom.

Maybe you should challenge my dad to a duel.

I don't want to fight your dad.

How come?

I don't know, I just don't.

They were passing the bottle back and forth. What's wrong? asked Eli; don't you like to fight?

Why would I like to fight?

Your mama likes to.

She's a woman.

That don't make sense.

Loren turned red, because he realized that too.

I just meant she's an adult.

That don't make sense neither.

I just don't like to fight, then.

You wanna fight me for practice?

Why? Are you mad at me?

No, dumbass, I'm trying to help you.

I don't need practice if I never get in a fight.

Eventually you'll have to have a fight.

Not if I don't want to.

You can't be a man if you've never fought.

I'll wait till I'm older, when I'm eleven or twelve.

Eli thought about it. That's awful old for your first fight, he said.

But there's nobody I want to fight.

What about your papaw?

You can't fight your own family.

That's the dumbest thing you've ever said.

Loren thought about it and agreed it was pretty dumb.

You want me to fight him instead?

A fight between Eli and Papaw was a strange thing to imagine, but as long as Loren didn't have to participate in it himself, he wouldn't mind if it happened.

I'll knock his lights out, said Eli. I'll knock him clear to next week.

Just don't let him know I said it was okay.

You wanna know what else my dad told me about her?

Are you trying to get me to fight your dad again?

No, I'm trying to figure out what he meant when he said it.

What did he say, then?

He said he's got more women than she'll ever get.

Sometimes Loren felt like Mother was hurting him on purpose by deciding not to be normal. She wanted him to suffer through what she thought she suffered herself, because she didn't understand that he understood her already. If that was the case, he didn't understand her at all, and they were back at square one.

Eli stood and balanced on the log barefoot. Cross-elbowed, he took off his shirt and tossed it down. He took his shorts off too. Completely naked, he jumped into the green water. Hell that feels good, he said, and when he stood up, the pond came only to his waist. There was something magical about Eli. Water dripped from his nipples, glimmering in the sunlight. Here I was, drifting above the two of them. I'd been there all along. I'm never far from Loren. I never disappear. I don't think such a thing

is even possible. Now, though, I was paying close attention. I'd
dreamt of a time when Loren would come to understand someone, to know him, and vice versa, and when I'd envisioned it, it
had happened this same way, but as I hovered in the stagnant air
I wasn't happy for Loren. I hoped Eli would remind him of me.
Eli looked the way Loren had imagined I'd look if I had a body.
He was throwing mud and letting it dribble down his arms, and
Loren watched, fascinated, hoping Eli wouldn't slip in the mud
and drown. People were supposed to wait an hour after drinking before they swam. If Loren was still thinking thoughts about
drowning, though, it was hopeless. That made me feel better. I
floated in a space that wasn't quite audible and whispered again
and again, Think of me, until I saw the futility of that act.

Toss me the bottle.

Come and get it. You'll lose it in the pond.

He wasn't scared to say no to Eli anymore. The wine made
him confident, he realized, and Eli came ashore and put on his
shorts and balled up his shirt and pitched it into the weeds.

Now the next guy'll have something to dry himself with.

What next guy? said Loren.

Hell if I know.

Do people swim here often?

Where do you come up with all these damn questions?

Loren shrugged. Won't Ruby know we're drunk?

I don't care; she's not my mom. She's as related to you as she
is me.

She'll smell our breath.

Drunks can never tell when someone else is.

Ruby's not a drunk.

When have you ever seen her not drunk?

I don't believe you.

Eli stopped. What does my breath smell like?

Loren smelled it, but it didn't smell like anything at all.

Okay then, Eli said, and that meant it was time to go. Loren followed and never thought of anything that wasn't really happening or any idea he thought might seem strange to Eli. They took a shorter trail than the way they'd come. Loren's head rolled forward with their motion toward the house. He was in tune with his body, and it felt good to move, and to walk behind Eli watching the small of Eli's back as they carved a path. He made himself look away. In a patch of skunk cabbage under an ash tree he saw a black and yellow snake. Red on black, a friend of Jack; red on yeller, kill a feller. That was what they said about snakes. Black and yellow meant nothing, and he looked back at his cousin and moved forward.

Eli, do you know what happens at a turkey shoot?

He knew it was a stupid question that didn't relate to anything they'd been discussing, but he felt brave. He'd formed a new theory about how to keep people from making fun of him: he'd say what he felt like saying, all the time, and stop worrying. Plus, not knowing about turkey shoots had been bothering him forever. Even Mother had refused to answer. He thought they might be the key to everything he didn't understand.

It's a big secret, said Eli. They don't let you inside till you're part of their secret society.

So there's no way to find out?

Eli shook his head. I know what happens, though.

How do you know?

Because I know everything.

He turned to face Loren, took a dogwood sapling in his hand, and pulled it straight out of the ground, roots and all.

What did you do that for?

They suck each other's dicks. That's the secret. That's why your mama ain't no different from everybody else round here.

Who told you that?

That's what it is they don't want you to know.

Why do they take their guns, then?

Have you ever seen anybody take a gun to a turkey shoot?

Cass took his gun to the last one.

That's to keep you from knowing what goes on.

Where do they have them?

In people's houses. Eventually they'll have one at Cass's.

Why do they call it a turkey shoot?

If you're too dumb to figure it out, I certainly won't tell you.

From now on, Loren would pretend to know everything. As far as he could see, no one understood what anyone else was saying, but they always claimed to, and so would Loren. He took a wild cherry sapling in his fist and pulled it out of the ground as Eli had, and threw it down to trample it when he walked on.

What'd you do that for?

I just felt like it.

Eli laughed. You're funny, he said. Sure you don't want me to teach you how to fight?

Loren shrugged. Maybe later, he said. Might as well keep on walking.

It was another mile to Ruby's. As they walked they spoke about the shittiness of Blount County compared to the fun of the big city. In Knoxville there wasn't nearly so much good-for-nothing land being wasted on useless trees. Although Eli hated his father, he liked that Dusty knew how to develop land and cut down trees. Eli already knew how to drive a bulldozer, he said, and when he turned eleven, Dusty would pay him fifty bucks a day to knock trees down. He'd use the money to run away and fly F-16's, not in the Air Force but on his own. They discussed the kids in Miss Rathbone's class, who would shit bricks when Eli buzzed the school in an F-16 and blew it up with laser-guided bombs and AGM-65 Maverick missiles. Loren was glad to hear that Eli disliked everyone at school pretty much equally.

They'd seemed like good friends of Eli's. He felt thankful to Ruby for bringing Eli into the family and granting Loren access to him that other kids at school would never have. Now that Loren was learning so many new ways of behavior, he'd be well poised for his own paddling contest with Eli next school year. They'd be equally admired by Rudolph and Lyhugh and Leland and the other Leland and pretty much everyone.

Aren't you scared you'll get paddled so many times they'll expel you from school? he asked Eli. There's got to be some kind of a limit to it.

Is expelled where you can't come back never?

Loren nodded.

I thought that was suspended.

No, it's expelled I think.

Good, said Eli. That's the one I want.

Does it hurt when Miss Rathbone paddles you?

Feels kind of good, in a way.

How does it feel good?

Eli shrugged. Get paddled yourself, and find out.

Maybe I will, said Loren.

I'd like to see you try.

What do you mean, try? It's easy.

Let's see you get paddled, then.

What would you do if they expelled you?

Stay home and play Nintendo all day, plus I'd go to school at recess and stand on the other side of the fence and moon everyone and flip them off and yell cuss words. I'd beat Legend of Zelda in no time if I got expelled.

It was a good plan, thought Loren, wishing they had more wine. He hoped there'd be more at Ruby's, but at the same time he wished they weren't so close already. The day had passed so quickly. It wasn't over, though. He wasn't going to start being sad about the past's being past. Eli was talking, and he needed to pay attention.

You can learn way more from playing a video game than anyone will ever learn from that dumbass teacher of yours.

She's your teacher too.

I ain't responsible for that bitch. Take Rad Racer, you drive around fast trying not to crash. You learn it's important to beat everybody and be the fastest. That's more than I've learned from Miss Rathbone. I'd like to see her try and play Rad Racer; I'd kick her ass.

They talked about Chilhowee Mountain, how Eli hated it and wished he were back in Knoxville where things were flatter. There was no point to a mountain, he said. It was stupid that people were willing to pay extra money just to live closer to one. Pretty soon no one would be able to afford to live anywhere but flat places. That was fine with Eli, because the money paid by rich people so they could live near Chilhowee Mountain would go to him and Dusty, and Knoxville was where he wanted to live anyway, not Blount County, but he still thought it was dumb. Everybody goes on and on about that mountain, he said, but I don't see the point to it. I'd rather just look the other way and not see it. I hope my dad bulldozes it down flat.

What about your mother, though?

My mom? What the hell would she care?

Why don't you live with her, if you want to live in Knoxville so bad?

Hell, said Eli, if my mom can't afford me, how's she gonna afford to live in Knoxville? She lives in Bean Station, and that's where she'll stay.

They emerged from the woods in the meadow above Ruby's house. Downhill from this field the state highway led straight to Chilhowee Mountain, which Loren could see in full. He didn't agree with Eli's opinions about it. Eli didn't understand mountains, because he'd grown up too far away from them. They were a lot more important than Eli thought. Eli had strange ideas. He could walk shirtless across open fields without shame. Anyone speeding by on the highway could see that he was half naked. He seemed to bask in his freedom. He liked being looked at. What kind of thoughts would Loren think about the world if he'd gone through life wanting to be looked at? It was frightening to imagine that he could be completely different if just that one aspect had changed; instead he'd hidden beneath a mountain surrounded by trees, the roads winding in and out of a hundred hills so no one could see him. He wanted to be living in Eli's body and mind, but if that were the case, he wouldn't be looking at Eli, and anyway, what did Eli want; what was Eli ever thinking? He was getting ahead of Loren, down the meadow, flanked by wildflowers. He turned around, his shadow behind him, the sun on his skin.

Will you hurry the hell up? I'm losing my buzz.

Does that mean we're going to drink more?

Does that mean we're going to drink more? Eli repeated in a voice intended to mock Loren's. He turned toward the house and kept walking as Loren hurried to catch up. He saw three cars parked behind Ruby's Cougar.

Card people, said Eli. I hate their guts. Don't worry, they'll be downstairs.

Eli led the way into the kitchen, where he turned the oven on and put a frozen pizza in to cook. He pushed a chair to the sink, stood on it, and pissed into the basin—that was how men did it, he said, toilets were for women—then they played Kid Icarus in the living room, and Loren forgot he was hungry until he smelled cheese cooking and tried to make his stomach not growl.

Careful, yelled Ruby from downstairs. You burnt the house down that last time.

Eli paused the video game. We had a deal, he shouted. Leave me the hell alone and I won't screw up your card games.

I'm coming up there to smack your face, she shouted back.

Shove it up your makeup, he shouted even louder.

When he unpaused the game, his character fell into a hole and died. Broke my goddamn concentration, he said, and it was Loren's turn. Loren began his second life and ran right, smiling at the thought of Miss Rathbone sitting between them on the floor playing the game too. Even Loren could beat Miss Rathbone at playing Nintendo. She'd be pitiful at it. He focused on what he could learn from this game. Jumping from platform to platform, he would eventually attain the sky, where there was a prize to be won. It occurred to him that he'd never felt hungry until these past few days. It was a nice feeling. It would make sense if he were more aware of his body the bigger he was, but the opposite was turning out to be true. If he were Eli's size, he could take his shirt off and feel the ceiling fan blowing on his skin and be more aware than ever.

Ruby was climbing the stairs into the living room with a pitcher and two tumblers. I don't know *where* he learned to talk that way, Eli was saying in a voice that mocked hers. I'm gonna send him off to that military school like his daddy's been nagging me to.

That sounds morn more like the thing, said Ruby, having reached the top.

It's as good a waste of money as any.

Sitting there without a shirt on like some kind of animal.

As if you give a shit about me.

Oh, sweetie. I know I'm not the mother you've always dreamed of.

Which one of your magazines did you get that one from?

Just put the pizza on a goddamn pizza pan while you cook it.

Eli held his middle finger in the air behind him as she went back downstairs. Loren wanted to go peek at the card people, but the pizza was ready.

I get more than you, said Eli. You're on a diet.

You said you wouldn't talk about my weight anymore.

You sound so stupid when you say shit like that.

It would take a while for Eli to get used to not making fun of him. The transition might take a couple of days. In the meantime, he might revert to his old way of acting, but that didn't mean anything. Loren ate two slices of pizza, knowing the whole time he'd quit after those two slices. They didn't even taste good. Maybe no food would ever taste good again.

The game was over. Are you done with the pizza? asked Loren. I'll put the rest in the refrigerator.

The hell you will. Just leave it on the floor; that'll piss her off.

I don't want to piss her off.

Let's go down and get some of her iced tea.

I don't like tea.

Well you'll like this tea.

So they went downstairs. Ruby and three other women, their hair in buns, sat around a wooden card table in the den, all with drinks. Hello ladies, said Eli, I've always wanted to learn bridge. Why don't you show me and Loren how to play?

He took two glasses from the cabinet behind the wet bar and filled them with ice. To have room to set the glasses down, he had to push aside a stack of blueprints.

Six cain't play bridge. Get your grubby hands off those papers. All that you are is destruction. Lorn, don't you look at those either.

We just want some of your tea, Mom.

You hate my tea. There's spirits in it.

Spirits, Eli said in a high voice. Oh my goodness.

Don't call me Mom if it's only when you want something.

He took a pitcher from the little refrigerator under the bar.

Loren knew it wasn't tea, but he didn't see why they persisted in calling it tea. Who did they think they were fooling?

I hope you've got more somewhere, because me and Loren are fixing to use this batch up.

Eli filled his own glass, then Loren's. Before Ruby could do anything about it, he had drunk what he'd poured for himself and refilled his glass to the brim. You didn't believe me, did you? You're so used to your stupid family, you don't trust a word anyone says.

Ruby's chair fell down behind her as she tried to raise her leg, but she hit it on the table and howled. When she finally reached him and snatched the glass out of his hand, he laughed at her.

You were right, he said, it tastes like piss.

I smell spirits on you already.

No shit. I just drank your tea.

He opened the refrigerator. What's in this bowl?

Green bean casserole.

It looks like turds.

Keep your hands off it.

I can see when I'm not wanted.

He walked past Loren to the sliding glass door and went outside. Loren wanted to follow, but he had the whole course of his life to think about. He might have to live with Ruby for the rest of eternity. Maybe he could make fun of these women behind their backs, and Eli would admire him for it, but he needed to be polite to their faces. Eli had shut the door anyway and couldn't hear him through the glass. He tried to think of something polite. He was supposed to call the ladies *ma'am*—Mother's least favorite word—but not if there was nothing to say.

Don't just stand there gaping at us, said Ruby. You made your bed, now go lie in it.

It made Loren mad that she'd tell him to do something he'd already intended to do. She was far too oblivious to see that he was trying to be courteous; did she want him to behave like Eli? If so, that was exactly what she'd get. This thought scared him as he walked outside onto the back patio; he didn't want to have to live up to it.

Ruby closed the door behind him, locked it, and drew the curtains. Eli was leaning against the railing of the stairs that led to the deck. I meant to smash that casserole on the floor, he said, kicking at bricks stacked up on the patio. I had the whole thing all planned out. It was perfect.

They kicked a soccer ball back and forth in the backyard. The sun was getting low in the sky. Loren thought he heard the women getting up to leave. Sure enough, within a few minutes cars were driving away. Good riddance, said Eli. The curtains came open. Loren thought he saw Ruby ducking behind the wet bar, hiding from Eli. Spying on him. Was it possible that she was lonely? He felt momentarily sorry for her. It was as if Eli's life was a video game; he'd reached the end of the level and defeated the villain. Loren hoped she didn't blame him too. It had been Eli who'd hurt her feelings. You couldn't act hateful to every-body all the time; life was more complex than that. The soccer ball bounced off Loren's shin. When Ruby slid the door open, she was crying.

They came all the way down here from town, she said.

They're just a bunch of hussies, Eli told her. It doesn't matter. They're mean old bitches.

Her face curled up again. They're nicer to me than you are.

Why do you try make me feel so guilty about things?

Ruby and Eli could express to each other the exact things they meant. Loren had never been able to do that. When he wanted to tell Mother he loved her, he told her instead that her meatloaf tasted good, or that he was glad she'd taken him on a drive. He was selfish to have behaved that way. It was funny to think of Eli being the selfless one, but here he was, comforting

Ruby, who wasn't even his real mother. They went inside together through the glass door, and Eli stepped behind the bar to pour her a drink of vodka and bitters. He brought it across the room, handed it to Ruby, and sat with her on the love seat. She draped her arm across his shoulder and smiled as she wiped a tear from her cheek.

You're drunk, she said. Both of you. I hope you're happy with yourselves.

Loren leaned against the wall facing them and wondered whether to be afraid. He wasn't a part of their household and did not want to be noticed. Ruby tossed her arms up weakly and then chuckled. Dusty called the house, she said. He got in a fistfight.

With who? said Eli.

Daddy.

Papaw? said Loren.

Isn't that funny?

What were they fighting about?

Dusty says he's an ignorant old fart, said Eli. That's probably what it was about. I wish I'd been there to fight too. I'd fight them both and kick both their asses.

Loren kept his eyes on Ruby to remind her that she hadn't answered his question.

It was probably about the land, she said. Whole thing's pretty funny, don't you think? Goddamn Riverlake. Come here, she said to Loren. I want us all three to get a good goddamn laugh about it together.

Loren looked at Eli, who shrugged his shoulders.

Come on, said Ruby. Laugh with us.

Loren moved hesitantly across the room. He sat down on the love seat on the opposite side of Ruby from Eli. There was hardly room for the three of them. Ruby laughed louder. She was practically cackling. Eli looked worried. He laughed too, not to appease her, but out of nervousness. Loren didn't think he could manage to laugh himself. Although his throat itched, he swallowed and tried to obey her. His lungs shook with the fake emotion of laughter as Ruby carried on; then Eli got up to leave without paying any attention to Loren.

Don't you think it's funny anymore? said Ruby, but Eli ignored her and climbed the stairs. Loren listened to his cousin's footsteps move across the ceiling.

Well it's not all that funny, said Ruby. Seems Dusty may have broke his nose. Broken it, that is. You got to watch how you talk if you want the right people as your friends.

Is all Papaw's old land getting torn down?

It's a good thing you don't like the woods. If you was to care, if you was the type to go walk around and look at trees and birds and flowers and bugs and all that whatnot, I might have said let's keep some of it and hang on to it for the future.

Where's Papaw going to live, then?

Frankly I don't care if he sleeps in boxcars the rest of his life.

Where will I live if he moves in with you? You've only got one spare bedroom.

Probably your Papaw won't have much longer on this earth. I don't want to upset you, but before you know it, your Papaw might pass.

He doesn't seem like anything's wrong.

Your Papaw, he's been married so long he doesn't know how to live without your Mamaw. I spect he'll pass within about three weeks is how it works.

Ruby paused to suck on a cube of ice. You get married so you can combine yourself with someone which makes it easier to get by, she said. Until they're dead, which means part of you dies too, take me and Dusty. He makes the money, but I take care of finances. If I succumb to the scarlet fever and pass, he'll be helpless, and his houses won't get built.

Do you have scarlet fever?

I'm talking about old folks, Lorn, not normal people.

Does Papaw know he's gonna die?

Don't tell him, or he'll get all angry and sing his songs, which we don't want that. Best let him think nothing's wrong. How do you tell someone they're ready to pass? It wouldn't be polite, and I don't think it's any way to behave. Mamaw, she knew she was about dead, but wasn't none of us talked about it. We acted like she was just fine. Mothers, they don't like their children feeling bad about them, so when your Mamaw was hacking up that double pneumonia for her last month, I let on like I couldn't hear a thing.

Are you sad about her being dead?

Ruby thought about it. I spect I'll think about her fondly, she said, but it's best to look to the future. Your Mamaw come from before that Depression which you knew all along she wasn't gonna last forever. Not to wish harm, but when something bad like a Depression happens, it's progress once everyone who was alive during it is passed.

Loren decided to change the subject. Did you know Mr. Ownby when you were growing up? he asked.

I did not associate with the likes of that man when I was a child.

What makes you say the likes of him?

Do not be around that man. Do not look that man in the eye.

Loren didn't have to worry, because no one looked him in the eye, ever. They looked into the place between his eyes that didn't have a name. When he was little, Mother had told him he had a third eye that would open only when he wasn't looking in the mirror. Every time he went to the mirror to look, it would shut again. You're too late, she would say. It's shut. He'd tried not to get too upset, because she was joking with him and he didn't want to hurt her feelings, but he'd been young at the time, and even now it was hard to control his emotions.

I'm going to stay down here and drink myself some more bitters, said Ruby.

Loren didn't want to do that, so he went upstairs to the kitchen. He recalled that Mr. Ownby had indeed looked into his eyes at school, or at least tried to. Loren had averted his glance to the ground to avoid making eye contact. How had Ruby known?

He opened a tub of egg salad and scooped a bite with his finger. He filled a bowl with it, and then he dumped it all into the trash. He buttered a slice of toast and tossed that in the trash too, right on top of the egg salad. He did another one, forming an egg salad sandwich in the trash can. He cut slices of cheddar and a piece of cake and scooped two scoops of ice cream. They trickled together into the bag. Soon he was bored. The door to Eli's room was ajar, and it was dark except for moonlight. Eli lay asleep atop his covers, his open shirt restless with breathing. Loren tiptoed through the shaft of white light toward Eli. He held his hand above Eli's breastplate. His fingers were a magnet trapped in limbo between its field and the universe. This was not acceptable behavior. He went outside, ashamed. Chilly mountain wind carried beads of pollen that he breathed into his lungs. Pollen was weightless, he thought. It didn't make him any heavier than before. He watched the hills eroding to the south, an inch per hundred years. He didn't know what it was about Eli. He tried imagining Mother feeling the same way about a man, but could not. He and Mother needed to get out of here, live in a new place.

A painful meow seemed to come from all directions. It took Loren a while to see the tabby limping toward the stairs. Its coat was tiger striped with blood that stained the clover flowers red in its wake. He knew plants had no feelings, but he couldn't stop from feeling sorry for them when things like this happened, and for the other flowers that maybe were their mothers or their sons. The cat dragged its leg in painful jerks, and Dusty, who had just pulled into the driveway, came out to the deck to investigate. He had a black eye and a swollen nose.

Hey buck, he said, and then he noticed the cat and said, Huh.

We've got to do something, Loren cried.

Serves it right for digging in my garden.

We need to take it to the vet. It's in pain.

I've got just the thing to fix that up.

He wanted to shoot Dusty between the eyes. That was where everyone shot everyone. At his touch the cat slunk away, its stomach red, an ear torn, water in its eyes. Cats couldn't cry.

We've got to help him, Loren said again.

Sucker could bleed to death all day.

Oh my God, said Ruby when she came onto the deck. When did you get home?

You want me to put it out of its misery?

Please, yes, that would be just the thing.

Hey kid, you could shoot it yourself.

Dusty went to his Ranger. As soon as Loren saw a rifle in his hands, he shut his eyes; he didn't want to remember. When he opened his eyes again, the cat had died on its left side, and was bleeding, and he knew his attempt not to remember had been futile.

Thank you, said Ruby. That was an awful sight.

Are you drunk or am I just smellin things?

Sure I'm drunk. Everybody's drunk. What did you do to my daddy?

Loren didn't want to be upset about a nameless stray cat; this was not the time to cry. Crying was in the past. Anyway I had stopped causing any of his suffering. The cat wasn't an official part of his suffering. Things had moved on and gotten more complicated, and the cat was probably better off dead, so to stop from being upset, Loren went around the house and listened to Ruby and Dusty. It was amazing how he didn't exist when people couldn't see him.

I ain't done nothing to your daddy he didn't have comin to him already.

This isn't the big city anymore, Dusty, we're nice to one another down here.

Old fool tried to tell me she was incoptant to sign away her share of it.

Well, if you're at that hospital, I spect that's exactly what you are.

That bullshit's for her dumb kid, Ruby, it ain't for me. I don't need that shit.

Hush your mouth, we don't know where he's got hisself to.

He can figure it out, Ruby. He's smarter than that.

So then you can figure it out too, no need to go beating up old men.

Yuns is a bunch of country-ass hicks I ain't never seen the likes of.

He stormed away from her, carrying his rifle around the side of the house. Loren didn't have time to get away before Dusty saw him. They stared at each other.

This here's a twenty-two, Dusty said eventually.

I don't care what it is.

What kind of guns you got, anyway?

I don't have any guns.

Well, I'll have to talk to your mama about that.

Clouds of gravel dust billowed fifty feet high every time Dusty sped away. He had plenty of money to pave his driveway, but Loren suspected he liked the commotion he could cause with dust. It could probably be seen from the top of Chilhowee Mountain.

Lorn? called Ruby from the back deck. Lorn? You out there, Lorn?

Ruby wasn't his favorite family member anymore. She was falling to the bottom of his list. At least Dusty had called him smart. There was a difference between liking people and respecting them. He could hear Ruby slamming pans together inside. It was nine o'clock. He'd walked at least three miles over the course of the day. He could walk ten more before midnight, when the count would begin anew. There was a flashlight in the glove box of Ruby's car. It was time for his second journey of the day. He knew that the home of Carnetta Sledge was on the same road as Ruby's, in the valley of a different stream. He thought he could walk there in about two hours. If he had the whole day, he could walk clear to Maryville. He wasn't a prisoner. If he could free himself of the desire to remain here, he'd be happy— and although he wasn't communicating with me during this time, I was following him south along the ditch of the road, then east, north, east. No road in the county went straight for more than fifty feet. What Loren was realizing was what I wanted him to realize. I was tempted to put all kinds of thoughts into him. It made me nervous to wait for him to have those thoughts on his own. There was too much at stake. If he'd been scared of Carnetta Sledge's driveway before, what would he do at her actual house? He needed me as a companion if he wanted to get somewhere in this godforsaken world.

He was burning about a hundred calories for each mile, and the howling dogs of the hollows seemed to suffer along with him, praying for the return of things he'd known. It did not occur to him to thank me for splintering his life into these pieces, but I didn't mind; gratitude makes me sick to my stomach. To tell the truth—which I think is what people should do more of—it's a mistake that such a thing was ever brought into being. But this isn't my story; it's Loren's, and I'm the scapegoat, an evil force roaming Earth trying to help people who can't be helped because they can't deal with the fact that someone's in control, and sometimes that's me, and I can do whatever I want during those times—so I fell away from Loren, leaving him to seek what little moonlight made its way through holes in the hickories overhead. He considered how much light was denied him in this deep valley, where the sun rose twenty minutes later and set ten minutes earlier than it would have on a plain at the same coordinates. Over the course of a lifetime, that was a year of minutes. The valley was Loren's problem, its lowness. Why didn't it adversely affect everyone equally? If he was the cause of Mother's condition, as everyone claimed, he'd have caused conditions in Papaw, Cass, and Ruby too. Thanks to Loren, Mother would get along with them again. They'd all hate him the same and they'd welcome her into their shared misery. *Her*, he thought, as his mother's sad face floated in his mind. Something he'd never done before was to admit to himself what little he knew of what was happening. His mother was a pariah to the rest of his family. They looked at her as they'd look at a lake rumored to contain some horrible thing from the distant past. Peering into the murky water, they were peering into her, too, but they didn't believe in her, so it was discomforting to look at water at all and not know what was available to be known. Loren looked like a boy to them. Mother looked like a woman to them. She didn't think the right thoughts. She didn't eat enough radishes or carrots. She couldn't be trusted.

Private drive, read the signs that rose beside gravel driveways leading into the dark narrow coves that never saw sunlight. *No dumping. Trespassers will be shot.*

The driveway of Carnetta Sledge had no sign but the lettering that bore her name. As Loren ascended it toward a log cabin in the pines, he wasn't convinced he wouldn't be shot, but he went boldly to the door, not worried about how his weight made him look, just doing what his thoughts wanted of him. There wasn't a car in the driveway. There weren't dogs. Probably this woman had nothing to do with his mother at all. Sledge was a common enough last name, and if it wasn't, so what, Loren thought, failing to trust himself long enough to lose the courage to break into the house. Maybe the door wasn't locked. He didn't turn the knob. Instead he walked back to the road and opened the mailbox. He hadn't eaten in four hours, and it felt good to be hungry. He was glad he was so far away from any food. There were animals in the forest, of course, and berries on the ground, for this was spring, but he was determined to stick to his new diet. Among the advertisements in the mailbox was a flyer for the Primitive Baptist Church: *Are you angered by the Evils that purveyed the Earth?* Also in Carnetta Sledge's accumulation of mail lay a letter from the Atlanta VA Hospital. Loren had never been out of East Tennessee, but he knew Atlanta was the largest city in the south and maybe the country. People went there and never came back. Since Carnetta was clearly gone forever, judging by her mailbox, Loren felt no qualms about tearing the envelope open. The letter, from a Dr. Spivey, read,

April 3, 1987
Dear Mr. Garland:
Herein, a revised invoice as per our conversation of Tuesday week. To arrange at such short notice has required the rescheduling of my family trip to Hilton Head, and so I am adding the nonrefundable portion of my condominium rental to your bill, as, I remind you, you have agreed to. Please note also that according to the agreed-upon Standard of Care I will yet require a 2nd letter of

recommendation from a clinical psychologist, one who can adequately evaluate co-morbid psychiatric conditions, before I will perform the mastectomy. That said, I am willing to consider requirement A2 met by only ten months of continuous hormonal therapy (without a medical contraindication), provided that I receive your payment forthwith.

The second page was an invoice for $9,406.30, which was more money than Loren had ever heard of. No one paid that much money. It didn't seem right to have to pay money to stay alive. He held the sheets of paper, weighing them in his hand, considering their meaning. His family kept telling him that Mother's troubles came from his overeating, so maybe this was a doctor who'd keep him from overeating. That didn't seem possible, since he was far away, in Atlanta. It was a powerful doctor who could make him stop eating from all the way down in Atlanta, and he supposed it would be worth ninety-four hundred dollars. He thought he might like to grow up and become a doctor like that himself. But he had to admit Dr. Spivey didn't sound like a doctor who was planning to stop him from overeating. What the letter made clear was that Mother had been keeping secrets from him. Whatever they were, she'd thought it was best to lie to him. Maybe that meant he'd indeed caused her problem, not with his weight but with the desperation to cling to things as they'd been before. Even knowing in his heart that she wasn't there, he looked to Chilhowee Mountain and said, I'll be different and stop listening to Luther and stop crying so much and being sensitive, because he was a boy, and he had the chance to do what Mother wanted to and couldn't, and it had hardened her heart against him. Without telling him specific ways not to act, she expected him to grow into a man who'd carry her casket when she was dead, because he represented her to the family, which, for all intents and purposes, was the only part of the world. His mind ached from all this. He sat down on the bank in a bed of morning glories, and the few that hadn't shut at sundown shut at the sight of him. It was a good opportunity for him to act like a boy rather than a girl. They were only flowers, he told himself; they hadn't done it to hurt his feelings, that was pathetic, they didn't even have minds, and even if they had, who cared what a couple of pink flowers thought. But Mother liked to say it was the principle of the thing, and it was the principle of these flowers, on an earth that told its every inhabitant to do the opposite of what Loren desired, that forced him to hold back tears. So he cursed my name. His need to converse with me at all had convinced Mother long ago he wasn't of her ilk. The world wasn't enough for him; he had to imagine more. He was never satisfied, the way a man would be—so he cursed my name, unsure what difference it made, and shut his mind from me as if I'd cheat and speak. He cursed himself for having spoken to her of me, promising her he didn't care what she was doing or whether it made sense, because he could handle it, and it was a terrible thing to be alone here with these miserable comforters telling him it was his fault, not that he blamed Mother for his troubles. She had left him alone, but he was ready to forgive.

It did not surprise him that Papaw and Cass pulled up in Papaw's truck.

Wha hell far, said Papaw, if that ain't a pig in a poke.

What's a pig in a poke? said Loren, without standing up.

The crap if I know, I just felt like sayin it.

Whatcha doin there in all them pansies? said Cass.

They're not pansies; they're morning glory.

You like the pansies, then?

Loren shrugged. I don't much care one way or the other.

Your mama, she's always loved the pansies.

You figured out how to tell a joke yet? said Papaw.

I always knew how to tell one.

Tell one, then.

I don't know any.

Are you gettin in? We got to get our deer skinned.

Loren looked and saw a dead deer in the back of the truck. Have you been out on the nature reserve again? he asked.

We was gonna, but then we saw this feller on the side of the road there.

Why'd you go and tell him that for? said Cass.

I'm too old to tell lies. I got to be nice, so he'll plant me right.

I think I'll just walk back to Ruby's, said Loren.

Anyhow, you might not stay at Ruby's much longer.

Well, that's where I'm walking to.

Well to hell with you, then. Walk back to Ruby's, then.

As much as Papaw talked about being planted, he didn't seem to Loren like someone who'd die anytime soon. Ruby's logic hadn't taken into account the fact that Papaw looked like he'd be standing on their graves singing songs long after Chilhowee Mountain had eroded into a flat plain.

Loren waited until their taillights had disappeared around the curve to begin walking. For every thirty-five miles he walked, he'd lose a pound. His flashlight shone on the parts of the road where his steps would fall. He didn't want to trip over any dead deer. Cass had probably run into the deer on purpose to keep from having to hunt.

Also, for every day he didn't eat, he'd lose half a pound. At seventeen miles a day, he could lose thirty pounds a month. Plus he was getting taller; that would help.

It had not eluded me that he had cursed my name. I didn't quite know what to do about it. I was still reeling from it. I wondered if I even wanted to win anymore at all.

Loren found a walking stick and for the rest of the evening he planted it with each right step. Not a single car passed him. Maybe the world had forgotten. Maybe he was alone to solve his little mystery, though he knew his desire to solve implied a hope for satisfaction in the solution, and he didn't quite know what to feel. He felt sad for the trees that would be cut down when the new houses were built. He felt jealous of people like Eli who could curse their parents without caring. The letter had said Mr. Garland, but of course there was no Mr. Garland; Mr. Garland was the name of Papaw and Cass, and someday of Loren. When he had asked the name of his own father, Mother had said, Is my name not good enough for you? Not strong enough? You need a man's name? That was five years ago, when she'd still said whatever she wanted because she didn't think he'd remember any of it. Now that he was nine, he recalled pretty much everything anyone had said. If he reminded them of what they'd said, they denied it. He was making it up, they claimed. But if he was stuck here forever with his imagination as his only escape, why waste it by imagining real people, like his family? At one time he'd thought no one else imagined things, but now he realized they'd depleted their imaginations imagining what already existed. So many thoughts went unthought because no one knew how to think them. But Mother knew, and when they'd spoken of names, she'd gone on to say she was more of a father than a mother anyway, and she'd be happy if he'd think of her that way, it wouldn't be a good thing for Loren to have any other name, he was born of violence, which Loren had figured referred to her C-section, which was due to her ovarian cysts, which Loren wished he could feel too. He wished other people could live in him for a few minutes so they could feel his own problems. He'd accepted Mother's answer and never asked her again, because he suspected if she'd had a choice she'd not have wanted a child, nor would she have remained in this part of the world. He didn't want to bring these thoughts out of hiding.

He tried to think about something else. In the dark it was snow-
ing with the white petals of silverbell blossoms. All the trees that
shook their branches above his head would die. He asked that
they be forgiven for their sins and accepted into the kingdom of
Heaven, which was the sort of thought he needed to stop having
soon if he was to be acceptable, if Mother was to return. He
wanted to get it all out of his system right now. He told the trees
this would be their last season of flowers. They should try to
hold on to the petals as long as they could and resist the wind. A
terrible storm was forecast for the night, he told them. Winds of
forty or fifty miles an hour would attempt to blow their petals
away. It would be May in another two weeks, and their leaves
would be budding. He was especially sorry for the ones with orange ribbons tied around their trunks. They might not want to
spend so much energy on making leaves this year. He wanted
them to know it would be a waste of time. Better to remain with
their flowers and rest. He wasn't speaking aloud. The trees
didn't have ears, and anyway he would have been ashamed. But
he told them one last thing: he might be leaving soon, and he
wanted to wish them a painless death in advance, because he
probably wouldn't be around to comfort them anymore.

He entered the house through the patio door. Ruby was half-
awake, sitting on the couch in dim light drinking a cocktail. I'm
going to go live in the woods, he told her.

We're in the woods already, sweetie.

This isn't the woods, it's a house. And I don't like it here. I
don't want to go stay with Papaw, either. This is stupid. I'm not
some little child.

Why that's exactly what you are.

Loren wondered if people's hearts jumped every time they
said what they intended. No one except for Mother understood
how to answer a question. Even when she wouldn't give him an
answer, she didn't deny one existed; still he was mad at her for

having waited till twenty-five to give birth; she'd made him miss so many things. What had made her want to keep all those years secret?

Well, anyhow you won't be here much longer.

Mother doesn't want to sell our land. She likes the woods.

Nothing's gonna change from what it's always been. It hasn't changed for years. Gets more the same every day.

We used to go on walks through the woods all the time. She took me down to Roulette Spring and we picked blackberries.

I believe you. But it has to do with money.

If you won't tell me where she is, I'll go find her.

Honest, Lorn, if I knew, I've had the spirits that I'd just say it to you.

She has to have told you something. She left me your phone number.

She said she was leaving, and then she said that's all she'd say.

Don't you ever have any curiosity about anything?

No, said Ruby, looking at her empty drink, I'm pretty much satisfied by things how it is. That's what Avery couldn't never take, like it's some wrong with me to try and be contented.

I know she has a girlfriend. I've been to her house.

Well then I'm happy for her. Ain't it great she won't ever be lonely.

You're not lonely either, Loren said. You've got Dusty.

Maybe she'll stay run off forever, never come back here to the loneliness.

When will they start cutting down the trees?

It depends on how people is. But I would watch out in those woods. You don't want yourself bulldozed. Trees, they can sprout back, but you'd just be plain old dead.

Not if you pull their roots out of the ground.

Ruby gently closed her eyes. I'm just gonna rest for a minute, she said.

I've been thinking about what you said about Papaw. I don't think he looks like he's dying. I think he'll get by just fine without Mamaw.

Ruby had either fallen asleep already or she was pretending not to hear him. He was tired of talking to her anyway. It was past midnight. He wasn't the least bit sleepy. He thought he might stay up all night. He searched Ruby's shelves for a book to read, but they were all condensed. He wished he were the cat; then they'd be sorry. Dusty had wrapped it in a plastic bag and fastened it shut with a twist tie. He walked to where it lay by the side of the house and kicked it. It was already stiff. He wondered if animals everywhere got stiff when they died or if it was a special property of this place. He kicked it again. He pictured Mother lying stiff somewhere and wondered if he could call her Mother anymore. The word *Mother* was branded onto his image of Mother, and he couldn't imagine calling her by another name. He wandered around the yard. There was nothing to do in the whole world. The wind started blowing harder. The temperature dropped. He couldn't see the stars. Soon the storm he'd predicted to the trees was upon him. It split the sky with lightning, tore at the forest, scraped the windows, rained hail on the roof. Ruby and Dusty and Eli slept peacefully through it all, but Loren watched the whole thing. The last thought he remembered thinking, before he fell asleep and dreamed nothing, was that if Mother had made him, she'd created everything he had ever done or would ever do. It wasn't his fault; it was hers.

When he woke up, he found himself lying on the living room couch. He'd never made it to bed. Eli was playing Nintendo.

Hey shithead, he said, you're awake.

What time is it?

Let's go outside for a while before the bus comes.

What time is it, though? Are we late?

You don't want to come out with me?

I just don't want to be late.

Why don't you like me?

I do like you.

Then shut up about being late. I'm the one that lives here, and there's something I want to show you at the shed.

Eli paused the game and beckoned for Loren to follow him outside, and Loren did, still wearing his clothes from the day before. It was good that he'd have no time for breakfast. No reason to eat in the morning if he'd just get hungry again. There were people who'd gone for months without eating. He wanted to prove a point to his body. He needed enough time to show Mother what she was doing to him. It was good she was staying away, he told himself. He hoped she'd feel guilty. If she couldn't be honest, Loren would tell his body to stop feeling emotions for her. It was like freeing himself of a physical addiction. First he had to get her out of his blood. He had been excreting her in his sweat and in his escaping thoughts. He'd scattered her into the atmosphere.

The yard outside was littered with limbs and oak catkins that had fallen during last night's storm. Loren followed Eli to the pre-fabricated shed. The door was padlocked, but Eli had the key. Inside, metal tools hung from pegboard on the walls. The left-most wrench in a row of wrenches was three feet long and two inches thick.

My dad stole those from the factory before he got rich, Eli said.

What do you do with a wrench like that?

You sit it on a shelf.

Eli pulled a little bottle of gin out of his jeans pocket. You want a drink? he asked.

Instinctively Loren looked toward Chilhowee Mountain, but there was no window in the shed. The only light came from the open door. He wished Mother and Carnetta Sledge could see him here with Eli, living a better life than ever.

You know you said you'd teach me how to fight?

Sure, said Eli, taking a drink.

I think I'll take you up on it now.

Take you up on it, he thought. That was the way to talk. Usually he was scared he wasn't using idioms right, so he kept them out of his speech, which made him sound stiff, but not anymore. From now on he'd talk normal. He wouldn't sound like a hick, the way everyone else did; only relaxed, like Eli. They were going to have a fight. Loren would wipe the sweat off his brow, make two fists, and fight. They'd hit each other, dodge punches, knock each other to the ground. Loren didn't feel scared of this prospect; after all, the only consequence of the injuries he'd incur was pain.

You don't want to learn to fight.

Sure I want to learn.

Right now?

Yeah, sure. What the hell.

There's nobody you need to fight.

Maybe Leland at school.

Leland never did anything to you.

The other Leland, then.

You're acting weird.

Are you scared to teach me? Think I'll hit you for practice and break your nose?

When Eli hesitated to answer, Loren could see that his suspicion was correct. He'd witnessed enough arguments in his life to realize that the only reason to argue was to avoid things. If Eli were anyone else, Loren could have made fun of him for his apprehension, but there was no need; knowing that he could make fun of Eli if he wanted to was enough.

I thought you hated everyone at school, said Loren. Yesterday you wanted to blow everybody up with a laser bomb.

Laser-*guided* bomb, dumbass, said Eli, thus regaining the upper hand simply by possessing a superior knowledge of weapons. Boys were supposed to have learned the names of various guns and fighter jets automatically by the time they were old enough to speak. It was a subject Loren thought he might never master.

Fine, let's find something for you to fight.

I thought we'd fight each other.

Where's that cat that's been hanging around?

It's dead, said Loren.

Oh yeah. What else can we use?

How'd you know it was dead? Were you the one that hurt it?

What would you do if I was?

Loren shrugged. I guess there's not anything I could do, he said.

You'd hit me in the face, that's what you'd do. How can you learn how to fight if you don't know when to hit someone?

I would if someone tried to hit me first.

Why would they try to hit you? Because they don't like you. You have to learn not to like someone else first, before they even get a chance not to like you.

Then show me the best way to hit someone.

Eli shook his head. I don't think you're ready for that yet.

He walked over to the shelf and found a huge permanent marker that said *Magnum 44*. He uncapped it and held it to his nose and inhaled deeply.

Smell this, he said. There was a reason we came out here.

Loren took the marker from Eli and held it an inch from his nostrils. He breathed a small breath, which woke him up, and offered it back to Eli.

No, doofus, put it to your nose.

He stared at the open marker.

Do it or I'll tell everyone how much you drank.

Loren had slept only three hours. He sniffed the marker again. He wanted to be wide awake. Suddenly Eli was coming at him, forcing the tip toward his nostril, and Loren blocked him. Eli was trying to force the marker to his nose. He struggled against Eli as hard as he could. With both hands holding Eli's arms he pushed Eli farther and farther back until they were leaning against the wooden workshelf. Eli dropped the marker. When he stopped struggling, the force Loren had been exerting pushed Eli to the ground, where the marker lay in sawdust that stuck to its tip.

Damn, ass-munch, you're kind of strong.

He couldn't believe he'd managed to knock Eli down. He supposed he weighed enough to win fights, if he would learn how to fight. While he was thinking about this, Eli leapt up and shoved the tip of the marker into Loren's nose.

That'll teach you to be so damn strong.

It took him by complete surprise. He couldn't help breathing sawdust grains through his nostrils into his throat. He choked on them. The smell was overwhelming.

Truce, said Eli. Here, I'll wipe the black off.

He pinched Loren's nose with the sleeve of his shirt. All gone, he said.

You made me swallow sawdust.

Why don't you stuff some into my mouth too so we're even?

Stuff it into your own mouth. I'm done fighting you.

Fine, then, maybe I just will.

Loren couldn't tell whether Eli was being friendly or hateful. Either way, it worked out. If it was the latter, fine; Loren wouldn't be living with him anymore. If the former, he'd take Eli with him when he ran away. He supposed it was the former. Somehow this experience with the marker was the first lesson in learning how to fight. Eli was demonstrating to Loren a reason to hit someone. If Eli had been some stranger, the appropriate response, rather than sniffing the marker, would have been to punch him in the face.

As promised, Eli reached down, scooped up a handful of sawdust, and ate some. Loren could see him swallow; then his mouth curled up and he spat the rest out. That's awful, he said. You should have beat me to a pulp for making you eat that.

Together they walked through the morning fog to the driveway where the dead cat lay in its garbage bag by the monkey grass. You missed it, said Loren. Your dad shot it last night.

He wanted to stomp on the corpse of the cat and crush it, not just to impress Eli further but also because he wanted to. In the end, he only stared.

I hate cats. Only good cat is a dead cat.

What do you hate so much about cats?

Cats is for girls, plus they're stupid and they stink.

Loren poked at the bag with his foot. I hate them too, he said. He imagined hurling the bag across the yard as far as he could throw it, but he wasn't fast enough; Eli did it first, and Loren didn't even feel like apologizing to the cat. It didn't exist, it was dead, it couldn't speak English, and no sympathy Loren felt would reverse its fate. He needed to make a list of all the things like cats that were for girls and not boys, so he could hate them all. Long hair, flowers, nice things in general, empathy, logic; it would be a long list. It occurred to him that this was exactly what Mother wanted. She was preparing him for the new reality. She didn't think he'd be ready for a shift in how to live, what to say, what to cry about. Just as they reached the bottom of the drive, the bus came. Kids were laughing when Loren boarded it, and Eli whispered something to someone that Loren couldn't hear. He sat alone near the front and closed his eyes. It would have been presumptuous to sit by Eli so soon after they had become friends. Anyway, Loren wanted to be alone with his thoughts. He watched girls chattering to each other about girl things and hoped what Cass had hoped for Delia: that they'd crust up and die. He didn't really hope it, but he made it known to his mind that that was what he was thinking. In this manner he'd see to it that his mind got used to its new reality. At school, waiting for the morning bell, he sat in the lunchroom with the rest of Miss Rathbone's class, but Eli sat across the room with fifth-graders. Loren lowered himself onto a seat across from Leland, next to Lyhugh, who turned to him and said, What in the hell? with long spaces between his words to get everyone's attention. Been tryin to get high? That shit is all over your nose.

He's all embarrassed at it. Look at him.

Loren rubbed himself to feel for black places. He couldn't go to the bathroom to wash them off, because he didn't have a hall pass. He didn't have a bandage to cover them.

Dude won't even talk. Probly still too high.

Loren hadn't known the marker would be there until Lyhugh reached for his backpack, but then he knew. The silver reflected the harsh fluorescent light from overhead. Mr. Mashburn was patrolling the cafeteria with the lunchroom ladies as Eli grinned and pointed from across the room. Loren imagined himself in Eli's body, seeing himself. He didn't care what he looked like. That was how he looked to people who didn't care.

I mean it, Leland said. You're in mega trouble.

Loren's throat was dry, but only because he was thirsty. It wasn't from fear. Everyone got quiet as they watched Loren and Mr. Mashburn, back and forth. He wondered if they were jealous of him, as he'd been of Eli when Eli had been paddled. Suddenly Mr. Mashburn was behind them snatching the marker out of Lyhugh's hand.

Now who does this belong to? he shouted.

All I done was touched it, said Lyhugh, to get it out.

Are all yuns deaf, whose is this thing?

Loren, although he was nervous, managed to keep his heart-beat under control. He hoped his courage wouldn't go unnoticed by the other boys. Just two weeks ago, he'd have had a heart attack and died, and everyone would have thought it was because he was fat. He found himself lifted from the ground, not by death or angels but by sweaty hands that carried him by his armpits to the office, where once again he faced Ronald Reagan in a metal frame beside the American flag. The eight-o'clock bell rang. He was missing spelling class, but he already knew how to spell everything. He tied and untied his shoe for longer than it seemed a school-day should last, but then the secretary said the principal was ready, and Loren let himself be beckoned into a swivel chair.

Did you do it? said Mr. Ownby in his office. Because either you did or you didn't.

The principal stared at a crack in the whitewashed cinderblock wall as tiny bugs crawled from it, smaller than lice. He held his finger toward one as if to crush it, then folded his hands on the desk and faced Loren, waiting for an answer.

It's hard to explain, said Loren. He wondered if he should be calling Mr. Ownby *sir,* but *sir* wasn't a word he knew how to say.

Mr. Ownby paused for a good while. You know, he said more slowly, touching a finger to his teeth as he spoke, I guess we may have to shut down the whole school for a few days, so the exterminators can come.

That's interesting.

You'd like that, wouldn't you? You hate it here.

Not any more than anywhere else.

Your file says you're smart. Course dumb kids hate it too. Can't tell kids apart that way.

Loren put a finger to his wrist to feel his pulse. Are you listening to me? said Mr. Ownby, scraping something—perhaps one of the bugs—from beneath his thumbnail.

I don't have my fingers in my ears, if that's what you mean.

I know what it's like to have to deal with someone like your mama. I've had dealings with people like that in the past, too, and it leads to some confusion.

People like what? That's all anyone ever says about her.

That's because she's like that. You can try to wish she was different, but she's not. It gets to where nothing she says makes sense, you think she's telling you the opposite of what she's telling you, because she thinks she's someone who can say the things she says when really she's something else, so you don't have the first clue how to behave, or what she wants.

So what is it you're trying to tell me?

Mr. Ownby shrugged. I'm just trying to figure it out for myself, he said.

When's the last time you've talked to her, anyway?

I guess it's been a good nine years or more.

Then leave me alone about it. You don't know anything at all.

I guess we'd best just send you on to class.

What should I tell Miss Rathbone? She'll want to know what happened.

Don't go, then. Just go on home.

Really? said Loren.

No, not really.

Mr. Ownby started to smile as Loren's eyes changed. It wasn't a smile of pleasure, as far as Loren could tell, but of knowing something he'd predicted would happen had happened.

How many miles do you live from here?

Three. Four, maybe. I don't know.

You don't know where you live?

No, said Loren, as a matter of fact I don't.

Mr. Ownby swallowed and peered through a gap in the blinds. You wanna know a secret? he asked. I guess you're smart enough I can tell you.

Whatever this secret was, Loren had the feeling it might change his whole life. He'd been aware for a long time that he didn't know certain things about the world. He knew most things, but there were two or three essential things he still didn't know.

All those bomb threats last month.

What about them? asked Loren.

It didn't hurt anybody, of course.

Because there wasn't a bomb.

I mean it was so warm and sunny out there, it being the spring and all. The weather's so nice in April. Didn't you think it was nice?

Loren gulped. I suppose so.

It was never in the rain or cold. I guess there was one day where the weatherman said thunderstorms, and I didn't do a thing, even though the sky stayed pretty, because I thought of lightning. As awful as it was to sit here at this desk, with these bugs marching out of a crack in the wall from the moment I arrive in the morning until the moment I leave, the last thing I need is for some kid to get hit by lightning and then me get blamed. I can't shoulder any more responsibility in this lifetime. So if you get run over on your way home, it's not my responsibility.

It's mostly through the woods anyway.

There's other things. Bear traps, and I guess bears.

I think they've mostly killed all the bears.

Three miles, said Mr. Ownby. I remember when I could walk three miles.

Loren felt silly to have gotten worked up about what Mr. Ownby's secret might be. There wasn't any possible way Mr. Ownby could know anything about Loren that Loren didn't know. All he was was the principal of a school.

Will you give me a written note, in case someone stops me?

Mr. Ownby looked down at his desk, opened his eyes a little wider, and began to stare blankly. Surely he wasn't looking for paper to write on. All over his desk were letters, report cards, envelopes, permission slips. He had all the paper he could need.

I didn't care one bit for your aunt or your uncle when I was in school, he said, but I liked Opal. What I said about dealing with people, well, she wasn't like that yet.

Hearing this, Loren knew he had to seem indifferent. It was a chance to put what Eli had taught him to use. Rather than looking at Mr. Ownby, he gazed at the corn plant in the corner of the office, still housed in the black plastic pot it had come in. The floor below it was stained, because no one had bothered to put it in a dish to collect water. That was assuming it had ever been watered at all. Every leaf had the same brown encrustation at the edges.

They'd just built the school about ten years before I was born. They used to put everyone from kindergarten to high school in the same building back then. We've got more people living in these parts than there used to be.

Loren could feel Mr. Ownby pleading with him to make eye contact. The place between his eyes burned from the weight of Mr. Ownby's stare. He knew the last thing he'd do would be to oblige Mr. Ownby, so he focused intently into the corner, unable to decide whether or not the plant was dying. It was anybody's guess. Loren supposed it was managing to eke out an existence.

Before this school, I don't know what they did. I suppose there must have been a different school, but I've never seen it around.

The plant was the only decoration in the office. Mr. Ownby didn't have any pictures of family members at his desk. Hanging on the wall was a framed certificate from the Board of Education, and nothing else. Dying was a relative term. Once something was fully grown, whether it was a corn plant or a cat or the principal, it had already begun to die.

We was in the same grade, me and her. I guess that's why I didn't like the others as much; they were in different grades than I was.

Mr. Ownby was speaking so tentatively that Loren almost felt like telling him it was okay to continue his story. He liked the idea of hearing stories about the past, especially since no one ever told any. He was supposed to be scornful of stories, though, and anyway his new behavior was turning out to be a success, so he kept quiet.

I thought if I hung around Opal and treated her nice, she'd like me, but she was the same to me as to everybody else. This was around the twelfth grade. Most people dropped out before that, but I stuck it out till the end.

Loren would drop out of school, he thought. The fourth grade was almost over. He would be a juvenile delinquent who learned things on his own.

That was before they put all these roads in, said Mr. Ownby. They hadn't dammed the river yet. There were all kinds of roads that got buried. Course, you couldn't go over the mountain back then; you had to go around it.

Loren shifted in his seat to show that he was bored, which wasn't the case, but he had learned that it was possible to tell lies without speaking.

I guess you don't know what I'm talking about.

Loren shrugged. He looked at the door.

I guess you'd best get going.

What was she like when she was little?

He thought about it. She was the type that knew which flowers were which, he said.

Loren waited for more. What else? he said finally.

It's hard to remember. Once folks change, you just think about them the new way from then on. That's been my experience, anyhow.

I remember people from before they change.

You won't once you grow up. However you are now, I expect sooner or later you'll turn out like everybody else.

He leaned across his desk, squinting at Loren. It made Loren uncomfortable to be examined so closely. Wait there, Mr. Ownby said. I'll be right back.

Loren anticipated nothing this time. Mr. Ownby left the room, shutting the door behind him. Soon he'd return through the same door. Nothing would change.

He came back with a wet rag in his hand. Walking up to Loren, he squeezed a few last drops of water out of it, then paused two feet away. Here, he said, but he only stood there looking out the window. The blinds were barely open, and there was nothing to be seen except for the same parallel slivers of the parking lot as always. Finally he leaned toward Loren to wipe the black marks off Loren's nose and lip. Loren had forgotten they were there. In fact he'd never seen them. They might not exist at all. Now that Mr. Ownby was rubbing the cold washcloth against his skin, he'd never know the truth.

Well. That got a little of it, anyway.

Thank you, said Loren.

Well, said Mr. Ownby, and sat back down.

Was there something else you were going to tell me?

He stared across the desk. About your mother?

Or whatever you wanted to say.

No, said Mr. Ownby. I reckon I've pestered you long enough.

Then will you give me that note now?

Mr. Ownby tore a sheet of paper in two and scrawled something illegible on the bottom half. Here, he said. Safe passage through the lands.

He watched his desk drawers for a moment as though they were his best friends, then looked up. I'm ready that you should leave now, he said.

Without saying good-bye, Loren stood up, walked through the office door, past the secretary, down the hall, out the front door of the school, through the yard, and then across the state highway, running now, jumping across a low place in the barbed-wire fence across the road, darting across a cow pasture. He made it to the woods in a minute flat. He ducked between two wires of the fence on the far side of the field and scraped his back on a barb. He hoped the cut would form a scar. He'd never gone home on his own before. It wasn't home anymore, anyway. Climbing a rock hill, he felt in his bones that he walked westward, his stomach empty, his mind clear of all the old things. A forest surrounded him. Soon it too would be destroyed. When a deer ran away from him between two hemlocks and out of sight, Loren wished for it to be running toward the national park, so it would be safe from hunters. Not that such things mattered to him anymore. Maybe they did a little, but not really. He wondered what Mr. Ownby had been talking about in the office. Perhaps Mr. Ownby was worried that he was going crazy, and wanted to admit himself to the hospital where Mother was staying. He'd been asking Loren whether or not she was up there on the mountain. He just hadn't wanted to say it out loud. People liked to communicate using their intuition, which was a problem, since Loren was the only one around here who actually seemed to have any. He intuited that he'd wasted a lot of energy being scared his whole life, because no matter what anyone did to him, no matter how much any of it hurt, nothing would kill him. How bad could things get, after all? Every time something he cared about was taken away from him, he adjusted so that he didn't care about it anymore. Were new concerns taking the place of the old ones? He didn't think so. Soon he wouldn't have any at all. He continued through the woods past more trees and animals he cared nothing about, and soon he was descending into the little valley of the Garlands' land. Mr. Ownby's first name, he remembered out of nowhere, was Jonas. Clearly the man wasn't going crazy. No one actually went crazy. He stopped to think about the fact that his family had thought he'd believe Mother was going crazy. It made him so angry that he saw streaks of white light flash across his vision. The same for Jonas Ownby, who wasn't the least bit crazy. He probably just didn't have any friends. If he had the gall to tell himself Loren was in his same situation and would therefore befriend him, he had another thing coming. Anyone who named a paddle after Loren's mother would never be his friend. In fact, Loren could see now, Jonas Ownby was his enemy. He made plans to tell Eli about Mr. Ownby's secret, thereby causing it to spread through the school, but Eli had tricked Loren with the permanent marker. In doing so, Eli had been teaching him a lesson about how to fight. The marker had given Loren a reason to fight not only Eli but also Leland, Lyhugh, Mr. Mashburn, Mr. Ownby, and even Mr. Ownby's secretary, for her meager but complicit role in the matter. If six people had conspired to get Loren into the principal's office, Loren's woes over his whole lifetime had been caused by countless men, women, and children. It was thanks to Eli that Loren realized he had so many fights to fight. The knowledge Eli had conveyed didn't mean Loren would go rushing to tell Eli about Mr. Ownby's secret as a way of returning the favor, but it would be nice, he thought, to lord the truth over Eli throughout the foreseeable future, wondering whether and when to reveal it. It would drive Eli completely mad.

After walking for nearly an hour through the woods, not tired once, he emerged at his own house. The grass was high; two white trucks were parked in the driveway. Worst of all, the front door was locked. Two surveyors in the side yard were pushing stakes into the ground. Loren removed the screen from the living room window and raised it high enough to climb through.

Look at that kid. Breakin right into that house.

Hey there, kid. What's goin on there, bud?

Loren didn't scuff his knee on the brick ledge or break the glass. He stood alone in his dark living room and closed the window behind him. One of the men came to rap his knuckles on it. Loren looked down at the man's red hair and wondered what to do. The man looked more curious than concerned, though, and when he got no response he returned to his stakes. Loren went to the medicine cabinet for bandages to take to the woods, but then he changed his mind; his desire for bandages was a vestige of his old self. Maybe this was a good time to take a hundred painkillers and die. In heaven he'd figure out why the electric lines had already been disconnected from the roof. Just because Papaw said Loren would be moving soon hadn't meant anything wasn't a lie, but somehow it had come true. Loren set his backpack on the floor of his bedroom. He saw his unmade bed and thought about his sleepless night at Ruby's. He lay down to think about his next move. Soon he was asleep, dreaming of nothing. When he awoke, he was terribly thirsty. He didn't know if he'd been so thirsty ever in his life. How many hours had passed? He was willing to suffer. If water had had calories, he'd have denied himself water, too. He moved into the hallway. It gave him a strange feeling to grope his way through the dark to his own refrigerator. When he opened it, he was hit by an awful stench that nearly knocked him down. There wasn't any food left, except for milk, but the surfaces were covered with mold. Even the tiny rungs of the grates were black with it. He took the carton of milk out, opened it, and held his nose. It smelled the worst of all. It had solidified. He held it over the sink. When he turned it upside down, it fell in a clump to the opening. Little pieces dribbled into the sink basin. He ran water into it, sent the curds spiraling down the drain, and threw the carton in the trash, and that was that.

He filled a thermos with water, put it in his backpack, left the house, and walked toward Chilhowee Mountain. He was going to make his presence known. If Mother wasn't there, he'd go all the way to Atlanta, but the mountain was right here, and he figured he ought to try it first. Atlanta was two hundred miles away. It wasn't in the mountains at all. He couldn't imagine why Mother would want to go there and leave the mountains. He thought he could walk to Atlanta in about a week's time. For his whole life, people had been telling him he was stubborn, and it was time to live up to what they thought and be the person he was. He was nine years old. His life would be half-finished before too long. He'd lived nine years in the shadow of a mountain he'd never seen the summit of. The crest of the mountain was the top of the whole world.

The trees were ripe with buds. Spring made people healthy. His legs quivered in the wind when he squatted to shit, and he wiped himself with hickory leaves. If he'd had to do it this way his whole life, he thought, maybe he wouldn't have eaten so much. As he crossed through skunk cabbage to the creek, a mosquito bit his arm, and he wondered if he'd remember that bite after ten years had passed. He recalled seeing all those cars headed toward Atlanta when Cass had driven him home from Tellico Blockhouse. It was possible one of them had been Mother, or at least Carnetta Sledge. Mother would have slouched down in her seat to be unseen, as Loren had thought to do, since she'd created him in her image. Instead he had watched the scenery and sat tall. Carnetta Sledge would look like Delia. It was hopeless to try to remember. The only option was to forget the past and forge on. He made his way over the foothills. Branches of dead trees brushed against him and snapped, his flesh the weight that broke them. Crossing a fence meant he was on new land. The trees here weren't green yet; leaves budded later the higher he climbed. His muscles pressed against the insides of his calves. He struggled through a laurel hell and turned to make a switchback, and as the hours passed, he thought about his new diet. If he ate eight hundred calories a day he'd lose a pound every forty-eight hours. He repeated this to himself until the mountaintop was close, which he knew because the trees were getting closer to the sky. At a high clearing Maryville was barely a curled-up fist beyond the foothills. A red-tailed hawk swooped by, twice the city's size, and landed in the skeleton of a tree. Things were beginning to happen. The sun would set before too long. Clouds were clotting up as Loren reached a bald outcropping where he lay in the grass and thought of emptiness, trees without end, thunder galloping through his pulse, five seconds from the lightning. He wanted to feel as he'd felt at the pond with Eli. He drank what was in his thermos and wished he had more water. No matter what he took in, he was insatiable, so he was glad he'd transferred the feeling from food to water. Soon the moon would rise, and he would see its motion across the sky until the morning. Already he felt it pulling on his heartbeat.

He lay down on a bed of pine needles to rest his legs. Soon he was resting his eyes again and was fast asleep. If he dreamt, he didn't know it. When he woke up shivering, the night was black. He blinked his eyes; he couldn't see the moon. He could barely see five feet in front of him. He was alone in the dark, and no one knew where. Anyone who found him wouldn't recognize him, because he was a completely different person. He doubted his own mother would know him; it was thrilling for him, lying in darkness. The voices he could imagine. A spider darted across his shoulder, and he knocked its webbing from his skin and hoped he'd killed it. An engine rumbled in the distance. He wasn't scared, but he wasn't not scared, either. His feelings were doing something strange these days. He seemed to have forgotten how to panic. He could die of exposure. The only road on

Chilhowee Mountain was Foothills Parkway, and it ran along the crest. He felt that he was near the top, because the stars were very close. He hadn't realized he'd come so far. Bears and wild hogs hunted at night, and he stood and stumbled over roots and tripped and righted himself. He reached the road and turned downhill and saw a mountain ridge. He couldn't tell which way was which and prayed the next noise would be a car. He was scared after all. The mental hospital was either to the left or to the right. It could lie around the next bend or he could walk all night and never come upon it. His socks were sponges full of water. The car was an orange Firebird, and he put his hands in the air until it screeched to a stop a hundred feet beyond him. He saw two faces turn and stare. The car rolled backwards uphill. Are you alone? the girl said to him. Look at you. What in the world are you doing up here?

The boy and girl were passing a cigarette back and forth. Loren saw that it was Delia and Gurney Flinchum.

What in the world are you doing up here? said Gurney.

Looking for my mother. Where is this?

We ain't your family no more, said Delia. I don't gotta be nice to you.

Shut up, Delia, said Gurney. I'm about sick of your family business. Here, get in.

Gurney looked Loren over thoroughly. This caused Loren to look down at himself. His shirt was wet and stained with mud. He ran a dirty hand through his hair and felt twigs and leaves. It was appropriate that a homeless boy should look this way, he thought.

Are you gonna stand there gaping, said Gurney, or get in?

Gurney leaned his seat farther forward so Loren could climb in behind them. He sat down on the hump in the middle of the back seat. There wasn't a seat belt that he could see. He looked out at the night, the stars, and imagined sailing through the

window as the result of a collision. It didn't seem so likely. He'd
hit the seats, or the dashboard, and continue living.

He's one of them Cass folk, don't you remember it?

Gurney smacked Delia upside the head. She smacked him
back upside his own head.

We're goin home from Look Rock, Gurney told Loren. You
ever go up there?

What would he go up there for? He's about six year old.

I was already makin out with the girls when I was five.

Delia's shirt was unbuttoned. Where was you headed? she
asked.

Loren thought Delia knew good and well where he was going. She'd lain around Cass's house listening to the various stories about Mother on the mountain. She checked herself in up
top the mountain. She decided she needed some time alone up
that mountain. Looks like you done gone and sent her up the
mountain. It was possible Delia was retarded, but even then,
thought Loren, she'd be aware that he was looking for Mother.
Probably Delia had been to the hospital herself. Why else would
anyone drive up here in the middle of the night?

I was looking for my mother. I was gonna climb until I
found her.

Does she live in heaven? said Gurney.

Shut up, stupid, said Delia. You member his mama.

But he just said—

He's drunk as shit, Delia told Loren.

She didn't wanna stop, said Gurney, but they'll shoot you
up here.

People do not shoot each other.

Those two kids two years ago got shot in the head twiced.
Never found the bodies.

How in the hell do you know they got shot twice, then?

Loren's first thought, when he'd stood on the shoulder of

Foothills Parkway in the cold dark, peering into the dark car at these people, had been that the girl was Delia. Really, though, what he'd meant to think, and was implicit in his thought, was that she was Delia Sledge, sister to the woman Mother had run off with, which made her his aunt, essentially. She was more related to him than when she'd lived with Cass. She was claiming she didn't have to be nice to him because he wasn't part of her family anymore, and it was the most backwards thing he'd ever heard.

Do you have a sister named Carnetta? he asked.

Carnetta ain't part of our family no more. We kicked her out.

I told you I'm about sick of your family business, said Gurney.

We gave her three chances to stay part of our family and she wouldn't take it.

What did you do then, change her blood?

Carnetta? She changed her own blood.

Loren had ruined everything by getting into this car. It was driving him back down the mountain. He'd climbed this high to be driven back home.

Say kid, you like my new set of wheels?

It doesn't look very new.

Went and totaled that truck out on the 72.

I guess this is a nice car.

Say, are you from up north or somethin?

No, I've lived here all my life.

New York, or Kentucky or somewheres.

We've lived in the same house since I was born.

Well you ain't gonna live there no more, said Delia, cause your mama's havin her titties cut off. You'll be on a different side of the mountain. That means we're enemies now.

I want to get out of the car, said Loren, but it came out so quietly that they didn't hear. Gurney was already talking over him. Shut up the nonsense, he yelled to Delia, or I'll smack your head again, and this time for real.

I swear, she got the cancer to cut her titties off. Cept it weren't cancer.

Why in the hell would you cut your titties off?

That's the way it is with them Cass folk.

Oh shit, that's the one. Gurney looked back at Loren. Was you runnin away from home? Is there something you want to tell somebody?

Shut up, he don't get to tell us. We're his enemy.

I remember now. That was your uncle I was drag racing, when I wrecked. Dumb old son of a bitch thinks his Fords is so fast.

Loren didn't repeat his request that they stop the car. Now that he'd heard Delia explain why he wouldn't live in his house anymore, he could imagine clearly what it would entail for him to be let out on the shoulder of the road. First he'd have to find the hospital. He'd walk there. The sun would rise, and set. More cars would pass, and he'd ignore them. He'd die of thirst. Eventually he'd find the hospital, perhaps at night, in which case he'd wait outside until it opened the next morning. In the lobby he'd find the woman to whom he'd spoken on the phone and he'd ask her for Avery Garland; she'd tell him she didn't see that anyone was there. I can't tell you your mother's here, she'd explain, because she's not. Before leaving, Loren would thank the woman, because her words would be the truth. At every hospital until he reached the Atlanta VA Hospital and spoke to Dr. Spivey himself, his results would be the same. It was time to be more honest with himself. His first step would be to stop wasting his time on hospitals that weren't the one she'd actually gone to. It was good to have climbed the mountain, but now that he realized the truth about it, he was ready to return to his usual elevation.

See, said Delia, kid ain't gonna answer you, cause he's your enemy too. You offer to take him back to where he lives, and he's too busy being your enemy to be grateful.

It was fine with Loren if Delia wanted to be his enemy. Plenty of people in his family were his enemies; having one more wouldn't make much difference. Anyway, he'd decided he didn't like her long before she had come to the same conclusion about him. That gave him a powerful advantage, and there was nothing she could do to hurt him. It drove him crazy, however, for her to claim she had nothing to do with his family at all. Them Cass folk, as she'd called the Garlands, would be with her a long time, it seemed, no matter how many lies she told about kicking her sister out. She could be his enemy, but she didn't know what she was getting herself into.

I'm not the one who decided it, but I'm your enemy, Loren recalled me telling him back when most words hadn't seemed to make sense. I'd said it to be difficult, or mean, or simply because he was fat. All mysteries could be solved by his being fat. Now he looked back and could see that I'd had a reason to speak. It was too late, though, to bother figuring out what it was. Forgetting was simply changing, so that his memories were rendered irrelevant. This meant everyone in his family had been different at some point in time, which was hard to imagine and probably a lie. Once, he'd have asked me for my opinion. I'd provided him with thousands of answers over the course of his life. Not only were we not speaking, though, I was a creature of the valley. There was no way I could climb a mountain, he thought. He'd left me behind at the bottom of the first foothill. Uniquely at this time in his life, he was entirely alone. Having beaten one enemy, it seemed reasonable to expect to defeat more. Delia carried the same smug look through every curve. He'd fight her along with everyone else. He added her name to his list. When people told him lies, they went to the top of his list. Why did it bother him, he wondered, when lies were told? He'd told plenty himself, and not to just anybody. There were all the times he'd lied to Mother about eating all the peanut butter, or all the ice cream, or all the pecans. Was he at the top of Mother's list? No, lies mattered only when someone was trying to uncover the truth. For so long he'd been desperate to figure out what was happening. He'd come up against too many lies to count. There were so many fights ahead.

Those two kids who got shot? said Loren.

What about them.

When did it happen? Who were they?

It was at Look Rock. Just some kids. Why do you care?

He didn't know why he suddenly felt so sure that they had committed suicide. It meant he could wander the woods all he wanted without threat to his safety, unless he was a danger to himself. It also meant people had reasons to die, which he suspected was true of pretty much everyone.

I just thought maybe they killed themselves.

Like some kind of love pact?

Or maybe they were depressed.

Depressed, said Gurney. You know, you're disturbed, kid.

Delia whispered something to Gurney.

That ain't what I'm saying, said Gurney, but you're warped.

Gurney whispered something back to Delia as Loren rocked back and forth with the sharp switchbacks on Butterfly Gap Road. It would have been so simple to fall off the face of the mountain. The Firebird would sail through the air over treetops and land near Loren's home. In fact he was surprised he'd never before worried about a car landing on his house. He'd spent the hours of many an afternoon listing in his mind everything that could go wrong. Too late to worry about it now, though; it wasn't his home anymore, and in fact there was no need to want Mother to come back at all. Mother allowed gypsies and hicks to know more about his plight than he knew himself. He felt ashamed ever to have begged for her return.

Fine, you skank, said Delia, no longer whispering. You're my enemy too.

Loren directed them to Papaw's house instead of Ruby's. He didn't even have to think about it. Suddenly it was his clear course of action. Living with Papaw would be better than living with Ruby, since Ruby's house had already happened, and Papaw's was where he was headed. Memories were okay, but mostly he looked to the future. He had more in common with Papaw now than ever; spending time with Papaw might therefore feel completely different than it had felt in the past. He might love every minute of it. He might drop out of school and sit on Papaw's porch singing songs for the rest of his days.

You sure you're gonna be okay, said Gurney.

For God's sake, said Delia. Look at him. What do you think?

I don't want to be arrested or nothing if they find him dead.

Chilhowee was a small mountain, so it didn't take much longer to descend to the valley and reach Papaw's long gravel driveway. He had Gurney stop at the bottom of the yard so that Papaw wouldn't wake up. Since Gurney had met Papaw at the funeral, he agreed it would be nice for Papaw not to wake up. Loren thanked him for the ride and closed the car door. Gurney wasn't a bad person, and Loren hoped he wouldn't die in a wreck from being drunk. He wouldn't mind if Delia died, though. If they wrecked, Loren hoped the impact sliced the car exactly in half, so that his enemy Delia Sledge would fall to her death while Gurney coasted to a gentle stop.

He walked through the steep yard to Papaw's old white bungalow. This was the first time he'd come here since Mamaw had died. In fact he'd never been to this house when Mamaw wasn't here. She'd spent her life quilting in a rocking chair on the front porch. The porch faced the mountain, once visible over the treetops, but then the tulip poplar trees had grown too tall. Mamaw had asked Papaw to cut them down, and he'd refused. Cut

em down your own self, he'd said. They ain't got leaves in win-
ter and I reckon you know how to use a saw.

Mother had told Loren about this. She'd been seven or eight
when Papaw had first refused to cut down the trees. It was one
of the few stories Mother had told Loren about her childhood.
She didn't like to think about being young; it hadn't been a
happy time and she'd be thankful if Loren would let bygones be
bygones. There was the poplar story and the twin story and that
was it. Papaw had told her she'd had a dead twin that had died at
birth. It was a lie, of course, which was what made it remarkable
that the same thing had happened to Loren. He needed to be
keeping a journal, he thought, so he could tell everything about
his own childhood that it was possible to write down. To whom
would he tell it? There was no one, but that wouldn't stop him.
Already there were things he couldn't remember about being
three, four, five years old. His head would fill to the brim with
memories. The old ones would be erased to make room. He'd
never paid heed to his family's assertions that he'd recall none of
this after a few more years, because they told so many other lies,
but he supposed they had to tell the truth once in a while; otherwise lies wouldn't be lies. There had to be some truth, somewhere, to which lies could be relative. It was a simple law of
physics. Surely his family resented such a law. The nerve of the
earth to force them to tell the truth at least once a month, or a
year. How often was truth-telling required by the law? Once in a
lifetime was probably enough. Papaw's lies, Cass's, Ruby's,
Mother's, could all stand relative to a truth whose telling had
transpired long before Loren's birth, a truth Mother didn't like
to think about anymore and would never reveal to him, simply
because she'd felt unhappy at the time.

Tonight Papaw's chainsaw lay in tall grass near one of the
poplars that blocked the view. Loren could see the mountain
anyway, because the tree was just beginning to bud, because

a waning moon in the western sky was illuminating the mountain's face. He imagined Papaw's songs written on the slope. Who owned that land? It was interesting that Papaw was the only one aside from Loren who'd thought to ask such a question. Perhaps Papaw was selling his own land to have the money to buy the land on Chilhowee Mountain. That was ridiculous, of course. It would be crazy for Papaw to trade good land for a rock slope too steep in many places to stand on, and it was crazy for Loren to think it a possibility. The word *perhaps,* followed by whatever nonsense could drift into Loren's mind, was a trap that had snagged him too many times. Perhaps he was done with being naïve. Perhaps he had finally come to the right house. Perhaps the reason Papaw had waited until Mamaw had died to cut down the trees, after she'd spent her whole life wanting it, was that he considered it a good joke.

An orange extension cord ran from the chainsaw toward the house. He thought he could still hear Gurney's car creeping up the valley. Eventually the noise trailed away. It was of no consequence to Loren that Mamaw wasn't sitting in her chair anymore. As far as he was concerned, she was the catalyst of everything that had befallen him this April. It wasn't a reason to fight her, of course; it was a reason to thank her. He was a better person now, which didn't even matter; Mamaw was dead, and he'd seen her laid in the ground.

When he opened the front door, he heard Papaw snoring. He hoped Ruby's feelings would be hurt when she found him here, assuming she found him at all. Maybe he was becoming invisible. Was it being awake for so long that was causing him to have such thoughts? He moved through the house, listening to Papaw snore, not bothering to be silent. The door to the bedroom stood wide open. Papaw was lying on his back in bed wearing only white underwear, his chest shaking with each snore. It was interesting to watch. Loren stood in the doorway staring. From now on, whenever Papaw sang his songs, Loren would remember this sight. Having committed it to memory, he pulled the door shut; as he walked away, it creaked slowly open. This made him smile. He began to laugh out loud at the bedroom door. He looked across at the sheets that covered the living room couch, the embroidered Bible verses framed on the wall, the jar of seashells that was a gift from Ruby: all these things existed because they were funny. Loren was learning another lesson in how to fight. He thought back on everything he'd seen in the past few days, for that matter his whole life, that he should have been laughing at, and laughed. This didn't bring him pleasure, the way a book could, or sitting with Mother in the kitchen, but it caused him to move his body and remember the past. It made him stronger. He didn't need Eli to teach him; he was learning on his own.

He made his way to the couch and lay awake. An hour before dawn, the birds began singing. He hadn't brushed his teeth. His toothbrush was in Ruby's bathroom. She'd know he was risking losing his teeth just to avoid her. Through yellow curtains the sun rose over Look Rock, where he'd been, and now he was here. At Look Rock he'd have seen the first light at least fifteen minutes earlier. Dusk would have lasted longer than it did here, where it was blocked by the knobs. He did not intend to remain in this valley.

By the time he was falling asleep, the sun was shining on him. When he awoke, it had risen higher than the living room window. Ruby was in the kitchen. He'd been dreaming about her, and she drew him out of the dream. He needs to get use to some place in case this goes on forever, she was saying. There ain't any other kids his own age out here. He and Eli were doing just perfect and you're an old man and he'll feel disconnected.

Don't you feel disconnected?

I should certainly think not.

I reckon I'm gonna tear my driveway down.

Daddy, they're tearing your whole house down.

Nobody'd come and see me no more that way.

Your driveway is for when you drive to your house.

Not if I tear it up first. There's connected for you.

I suppose you'll dig up your septic tank and shit in the woods, too.

If I sold that tank, at least it'd fetch the money so you'd plant me right.

Lorn needs to get up and go to school this instant!

I dropped out of that school when I was eight years old.

You never talk about when you were a kid.

Name one time I haven't talked about it, Papaw shouted, the floorboards creaking now as he moved across the room, his voice rising. Every time I say goddamn it, that's what I'm talking about. That's what it was. Come back in here. I ain't done talking to you. No, I guess I am done.

When Loren heard movement toward him, he jumped up and went to hide in the back room before Ruby could find him lying awake. I guess he can just lay out all he wants, she was saying. They'll hold him back and he can repeat the fourth grade, all cause you're jealous of me for making something better of myself.

Loren peeked his head out the door to watch what was happening, just in time to see Ruby whisk the jar of seashells from the coffee table into her purse. Mommy told me what you think about these, she said, barely louder than a whisper. I swan to the Lord that I will not do anything nice again the rest of my time on this earth, you sad old I can't even say what. Rescued them out of the surf at Hilton Head, your own blood daughter. You'd have left them to be bulldozed with the rest of your house. I will not have my gifts buried under the dirt. I should have put them in her coffin, where they'd be appreciated.

Papaw sat down and took out his pack of cigarettes. Go get yourself a new pa, then, he said, flicking his lighter at a fly buzzing far above his head. He lit a cigarette, took a drag as Ruby folded her arms to wait for more of a response, and held smoke in his lungs forever. Finally he blew it out. Don't make those eyes at me, he said. Look at your damn self.

She unfolded her arms, got her car keys from her purse, and opened the front door. Good-bye, Daddy, she said in the doorway. Cass is coming for his deer. Not that I care, but he's my brother and he asked me to tell you. Treats me like a sister which is more than I can say of the likes of you.

You and Cass just mean the world to each other, I guess.

I will not grace that with an answer. Now that my mother is passed and you're on your way, Cass is all I've got left of family. I'll teach him to play bridge and you can sit singing your songs till you're nothing but a pile of bones.

She shut the door slowly behind her, holding on to the doorknob as she turned it, until the latch had eased silently into the strike plate. Loren heard the soft sound of her footfalls across the porch. He realized that Papaw was aware of him.

Reckon you got weary of playing bridge.

I didn't play, said Loren. I went walking.

It won't be no better here. Ain't nothing to do, your whole life.

I'll be okay. I just wanted a place to sleep.

Looks like that's what you got.

Loren leaned against the wall and waited for Papaw to say his next thing. Out the window he could see chickadees on the birdfeeder nibbling at thistle seed. In another life he'd have asked Papaw about birds, but in his new way of engagement he felt like letting out a string of random curses for no particular reason. He used to think people liked to be asked about things they were interested in. What a pile of shit that was.

You reckon this is how you want to spend your day?

I guess I could go to school.

That's the last thing you're gonna do, is go to that school.

Papaw drifted out to the porch. He knew more than he'd once seemed to. Loren followed him outside. Together they propped their feet on the wicker chest.

Why ain't you with Eli?

He shrugged. Papaw lit another cigarette. Loren thought of smoking one himself.

Go play those video games.

Maybe some other time. I'm okay here.

I've lived all over the country, said Papaw. Etowah, Chattanooga, Oneida—it's all the same. We got the same things here as anywhere on earth.

After a while Loren went to the kitchen, where he folded and unfolded a napkin, tore it to pieces. The house was getting hot; the ceiling fan was broken. He went to the living room; the fan there was broken too. Maybe it was how Papaw wanted them. He heard Papaw calling him from the porch, and he went back outside.

I reckon we're gonna play us some bridge ourselves.

Papaw took ten playing cards from his pocket, gave five to Loren—the two of clubs, the ten of spades, the ten of clubs, the jack of hearts, the six of diamonds—because it bothered him that Loren was bored, maybe, because it was his own fault Loren was at his house in the first place, because Papaw could have gone anyplace, thus causing Loren to be born anywhere in the world. Instead, he'd stayed at his house forever.

Bet me a bottle of gin, said Papaw.

What are we betting on? Where are the rest of the cards?

I gave you the lucky ones. Kept the shitty ones for myself.

I don't have a bottle of gin.

What have you got a bottle of?

Nothing, said Loren.

Bet me that shirt.

It wouldn't fit you.

It don't fit you either.

What are you gonna bet me?

Done told you. A bottle of gin.

Papaw placed two cards on the wood, the three and four of hearts, the other three unevenly in a facedown line. His grunt when he handed Loren a flyswatter carried itself through the valley. Papaw held his plastic swatter in his right hand, and Loren did the same. He spread his cards out in a crescent on the wood. At least five flies were in the air between the two of them.

How long does this usually take?

That depends on how good you are.

Something was broken down inside of Papaw, maybe in his feet. He sat still for five minutes while flies landed on the railing and lifted off. Loren had no choice but to do the same. For the first time, he thought he wouldn't mind turning out like Papaw. He saw himself sitting on a porch, his memories cloudier each year, playing fly poker with grandchildren, staring at Chilhowee Mountain as the world closed in around him. Once in a while the smell of cooked carrots would carry him back to childhood. The cherry blossoms would come. The scent of flowers in spring made Loren sad. He didn't know why, but it was probably because something was irretrievably lost to him. If he had to give up one of his senses, he'd choose smell, he thought, and with it taste.

When a fly landed on his rightmost card, he swatted and missed. You got to pick that one up now, said Papaw. You don't get to keep it no more.

Papaw raised his swatter high and gripped it even more tightly. He poured himself a sip of gin into the bottle's upturned cap. He swallowed and set it back down and sighed.

Reach for the bottle and see what happens, he said.

I'm not interested in the bottle.

Interested, Papaw said as if each syllable was sticking to his tongue like flypaper. Loren would take his flyswatter with him to school tomorrow. He wanted one that conducted electricity, even if it didn't shock people any more than spark plugs. The smaller people were, the harder they'd get shocked. Eventually he reached for the bottle, and Papaw swatted his hand.

You ain't won that yet.

But you're drinking from it.

Cause it's mine. I ain't tried to drink from your shirt.

You're not making any sense, Loren complained.

Sense is kind of like your asshole.

What are you talking about?

Papaw thought for a minute. I don't remember, he said. But it works out if you think about it.

Are you depressed about something?

Depressed, Papaw said. Depressed? Huh.

I'm sorry. I didn't mean to hurt your feelings.

I reckon if Avery can be so durn depressed, I've got a right to think some things too.

Have you talked to her since she left?

Avery ain't never liked talking to me much.

Does that make you sad?

Does it make me sad? Naw. I reckon she can do what she wants.

Flies could spend whole days buzzing around the same place. If they lived only for a week, why didn't they spend it seeing things? June bugs never moved fifty feet from where they were born. They died after one day. They could see the mountain the same as Loren. When he wasn't doing anything new, when he was only sitting inside a house wasting time, he felt anxious even with untold years left to live.

Bugs is about the only thing worth watching, Papaw said.

Think how it would feel to be one. Just buzz around all day. You could buzz right over that mountain. You'd see straight down to those Indians on the other side. You'd see clear across the county. I've been sitting here my whole life looking at these bugs trying to figure what it is they see up top of that mountain. Think how it would feel. Somebody else come buzzing up at you, all in your face like, you'd just buzz away. Say Ruby comes buzzing up at you about her tradition, she'd never catch up. She'd be too weighed down by that makeup to ever be able to fly. She'd be a mosquito is what Ruby'd be. Mosquitoes is all filled up with disease. There's places where you can die from a mosquito. That's what she'd be, buzzing in your ear and you're swatting at her, but she don't never die. And Cass, he'd be an ant. He wouldn't fly. He wouldn't be a bug at all. I reckon I could sit here and watch bugs the whole day.

He smelled the air. Wind's coming, he said. Get ready.

When the six of spades blew from the railing to the porch floor, it fell past a fly that changed its course and came to rest on the card's gloss. Papaw clenched his flyswatter, swung his arm, and crushed the fly against the image of an angel. Loren had lost. Papaw stood up, dropped his swatter into the bushes below the porch, and jabbed his hand toward Loren.

Gimme your shirt, he said.

You don't really want it.

It's the only thing I've wanted this whole week.

Loren felt that he was wasting away. He undid his top button and worked his way down, exposing his chest to the breeze. He took off the shirt and stood half-naked on the step, five pounds smaller than when Mother had left. Wasting away sounded abhorrent, but Loren thought it might be the best thing that had ever happened to him. And for the first time since his wasting had begun, he sought me instead of Mother. He spent a few minutes remembering me. Perhaps it was sadder to have lost me than to have lost her. He'd ceased believing in me, but now he tried to stop believing in himself, instead. I can't deny feeling jealous of the ability to be believed in. My jealousy and Mother's spiraled together into the little valley, for she'd wanted to stamp me out, and here I was, the wager having reached its final moments, when I suspect she realized that if she intended to cripple me, she'd have to keep making similar wagers for the rest of eternity. It really had nothing to do with Loren at all, which I think he was beginning to realize, as Papaw touched his finger to Loren's chest. His body went cold from his waist to his scalp. He couldn't close his eyes, nor did he want to. As far as he was concerned, he was an orphan, and I couldn't think of what to tell him to suggest anything different. He'd always thought I'd existed to torment him, but the truth is this: I'd only wanted to help. Now that he was a better person, he didn't seem to need me. I was a component of his memories, and that was all.

Looks like you just might have lost some weight, said Papaw. Looks like somebody went and ate one of them taters out of your tater sack.

Papaw ran his finger down Loren's torso an inch, then stepped back, the shirt in hand. In doing so he knocked the bottle over with his foot, spilling it onto the wood, which was kind of pathetic, and I had nothing funny to say about him anymore. The gin smelled like dried-up stalks of celery. Being near it and Papaw and the mountain and the land's end was changing Loren. He knew Mother would abandon him forever if he spoke my name. There were things I could have done to force him to acknowledge me. I could have turned into an animal, or set myself on fire in the form of a fruit tree. I could have turned everything backwards, so that water would flow out from under the earth, up the mountain, soiling the sky with its pollution; so that words wouldn't make sense, and men would speak in tongues, and the Black Sulphur Knobs would erode away, leaving so many holes in the ground. I think I could have ended the whole world. Loren would have died, and everyone else too, leaving behind only their urges, on which I would have continued to feed. I hadn't meant to start all of this. All I wanted was someone to play with. But Loren wouldn't allow himself to think my name. He considered that if Papaw were younger, they'd have been best friends, the two of them, patrolling the mountain like bandits, and there'd be others their age, too, but Papaw wasn't, so Loren went in the house and got his backpack and his shoes and one of Papaw's T-shirts. He went out the back door and around the side of the house. He knew there was a rusty old Schwinn in the lean-to, and he got it out and wheeled it down to the road, never having ridden a bicycle before. Given that fact, I thought I had a chance. You can't ride that bike, I taunted. You'll fall and break your neck. You'll never figure it out. You're way too fat ever to learn how to ride a bike. You missed your chance, Loren.

He pretended that my voice didn't exist. He fell off to the side. He was out of sight of the house. He tried again and pedaled twice before landing on his feet. It wasn't easy for me to allow him to believe I had caused him to fall, and that every bit of learning how to move forward was a defeat to me. He climbed out of the saddle and lost his balance and climbed up again and lost his balance and lost it about forty times before learning to propel himself forward. I rode beside him, on air, into the wind, silently. He made himself steer with his body. Halfway to school he wasn't falling anymore. It was sixty degrees, but he was sweating, and this wetness felt good in the wind that we'd—that he'd—created. He was risking everything with these pronouns. He knew he was breaking Mother's heart if she was watching him from somewhere; at the same time he prayed for her to be watching. He couldn't balance his thoughts, but he learned to balance his physical body just in time to coast downhill through Suicide Bend, and when he did it, every hair on his legs and

arms danced in the air, so that for a few moments he forgot the
need to abandon me forever and was borne only by the sensa-
tion of descent.

It was recess at school, and the fifth-grade boys were playing
shirts-and-skins. Loren planned to be thin once and for all by
the time he was in the fifth grade. He'd be able to play even if he
ended up on the skins team. Some of the kids in his own year
were crawling like spiders through the jungle gym. He walked
up to it. No one seemed to notice his late arrival, which seemed
fitting. He was ready for everyone to start ignoring him until it
was time to notice, and so he blended in, swallowing his fear of
heights and creeping onto the second rung of the outer rim. He
felt thankful that none of the other kids mentioned that he'd
never done it before. And he thought my name, just to see if
I was still there. It occurred to him that he might never be able
to stop thinking my name. We climbed to the next level. We
seemed to be as high as the top of the mountain.

I guess I should say— he began to tell me, but he trailed off.

Had he stopped because he didn't want to talk to me? Because the jungle gym faced Chilhowee Mountain? Because he
wanted Mother to return? I don't think so. Loren knew now
that everything I'd told him was true. I'd wanted us running
through the hills together. It would have been a great thing. But
he couldn't say the words. It's hard for people to admit their
mistakes. It's one of the most difficult things for them to do.
Loren had been through so much. He was changing himself
into the right person for me. In the face of that, what were a few
words?

When school ended, Papaw was standing beside the chain-
link fence that surrounded the schoolyard. His truck was parked
by the road. He was staring at the mountain. It seemed like Papaw was engaged in a lifelong fight against that mountain.
Everything he said was some attempt to understand it, but he

didn't know the first thing about it. He believed Indians were sunbathing on the other side of it. He'd never even seen that other side, which couldn't possibly be true, given how old Papaw was, but it was what he claimed. Here he was, even now, staring at it. I informed Loren that he'd turn out exactly the same way. Look how you're staring, I told him. You want to understand the mountain too. How do you think you'll understand a mountain? Who do you think you are? You can't even see it, I said, because by that point in the afternoon the air was so hazy that the summit was almost the sky's same blue-gray. Mountains don't have any meaning. I'll show you what that mountain means. You think you'll learn what it means from Papaw, or from me? Why do you stare at it so much if it blocks the sun? You think it's pretty? You like the idea of being on top of it, even if you never are? Even if Mother isn't, either?

Loren didn't answer these questions. He wheeled the bicycle to Papaw's truck and pushed me to the back of his mind to keep me secret there forever and save me for later, for a time that would probably never come, when we would be alone.

Just throw it on top there, I guess.

Loren smelled the deer before he saw it. The odor hit him with the force of a punch. He stopped in his tracks and clenched his eyes shut, then opened them, crept closer, and saw that the carcass was covered in moist sawdust. Some of its insides had been cut open and sawdust poured on them to soak up what blood had been there. Decomposition had begun, and there were maggots, but not nearly as many as Loren thought should be present.

Composted it too late to cover the stink, said Papaw.

Why would you leave a dead deer in your truck? What's wrong with you?

You gonna go and run away from me like that every day?

You expect me to ride in that truck with your deer smelling like that?

Not before you put my Schwinn in the bed, I don't.

Loren tried holding his nose with one hand and lifting the bicycle with the other, but it was too heavy; he had to use both hands. He breathed through his mouth, but the scent of death still entered his lungs. He got in the truck cab, and Papaw began to drive.

Now then. Gonna run away like that every day?

You saw me leave. You knew I had to go to school.

Turning out just like your mama.

If you're gonna say that, say what you think she's turned out like.

To tell the truth, she's run away too much for me to know.

You could take a guess.

I could whup you if I wanted.

I'll bet I could whip you, too.

My mama use to whup me every night.

Loren wanted to write down everything Papaw said and burn every last page. You told me your parents died before you were born, he said.

If that was true, I wouldn't have been born at all.

You said it though, said Loren.

So you wish I hadn't said it? You reckon you'd be better off if I went back in time and shut myself up whenever I've talked?

I just wish you'd tell me the truth.

The truth, said Papaw, rolling his window down, is my folks weren't no good. It was about like that mountain up there. Imagine if that mountain was your mama. There's things you want when you're a kid. You think I don't remember. Well I remember a thing or two. Ain't no kid doesn't cry now and then. Imagine if you cried and your mama was that mountain.

Loren looked at Chilhowee Mountain for about the millionth time in his life. It ran as far as he could see in front of him and behind. It was beginning to change from brown to green; soon its clefts and bulges would be mostly invisible until October. Its crest rose to a high point directly above the road currently carrying him through the valley; then it sank into a gap where Montvale Road crossed to Happy Valley on the other side. Butterfly Gap was visible too in the rearview, but this gap above him had no name. Back when Loren had asked questions about his environment that had caused his whole family to distrust him, he had insisted there must be a name for it, and someone ought to know it; this had resulted in shouting that had caused Loren to eat half a jar of peanut butter to comfort himself. It made no sense for gaps not to have names, he'd thought; how had the engineers who built Montvale Road distinguished this gap from others? Now that Loren was older, he didn't care, and it was almost funny to him that he could point to a particular pound of fat hanging on him for every element of his world that at some point hadn't made sense. He moved his eyes away from the nameless gap back up to Look Rock, which rose to its left. He'd never climbed the tower and probably never would, now that he was leaving. He could imagine the view: it would consist of the places he'd been seeing his whole life. The bodies of the two kids who'd committed suicide would lie on the rocks below. There'd be other escarpments on the way to Atlanta. Nothing was unique about this mountain. It was possible that everyone in Blount County was lying by calling it a mountain at all, and it was nothing more than a big hill.

You done imagined it yet?

Loren considered shaking his head, but nodded instead.

Well, that's what I was talking about. It wasn't no lie.

You said there's things you wanted when you were a kid.

Are you still calling me a liar?

What was it you wanted?

To get out of here.

Then why didn't you?

I did, said Papaw. You heard me on the porch this morning. I've been to Crossville, Cumberland Gap, Asheville. I've been all over. I've been pretty much everywhere.

Maybe if you'd gone farther. Maybe you came back too soon.

I reckon I'll know the answer before too long.

What do you mean?

Papaw stuck his hand out the window and felt the air. Loren thought Papaw was telling him he was dying. Papaw was going to kill himself, and Loren was the only one who knew. He watched Papaw's hand sailing in the wind created by the truck's forward motion. He hadn't thought of Papaw as someone who enjoyed a breeze, but here he was, letting it caress his skin. It was possible he'd driven to the school not to bring Loren home, only to create a wind that wouldn't have existed otherwise. It was his last act before dying. Loren thought about suicide. It was surprising to him that more people didn't kill themselves. He knew he never would, because there were too many mysteries to solve, but what about people who didn't pay attention to mysteries; why did they choose to remain alive?

I reckon I'll head to Nashville, Papaw finally said, and sell my songs. That's what I meant about knowing the answer. Everyone'll be sorry once they hear my songs.

Why will they be sorry?

Won't be able to turn on the radio without it being one of my songs.

Aren't you too old to start writing songs?

Loren was sorry he'd said that. No, he decided, he wasn't sorry; after all, it was what he'd meant to say.

I've been writing songs my whole life, said Papaw. It's all I've ever done.

How will you sell them, though?

You think you can take my songs and sell em yourself, just cause you're young? Go on, try and go to Nashville. I've been everywhere. It's all the same.

He pulled off at a wayside by a drop-off of at least thirty feet. I guess we'll stop and take care of our business, said Papaw.

He got out of the truck, walked around back, lowered the gate, and dragged the deer out with his bare hands. It fell in a clump on the dirt, sawdust all over it. Through the side mirror Loren watched Papaw trying to kick it off the cliff, but it wouldn't budge. Papaw knelt down and pushed it, using his back to give himself the necessary force. Finally it fell. He wiped his hands on a patch of grass and stood up and got back in.

Too good to help out your old Papaw, I guess.

He got behind the wheel, flooded the engine, shifted into first, and pulled onto the road. Loren rolled his window down to create a crosswind that made it too loud to talk. He was traveling at forty miles an hour. It was equally true to say the valley moved toward him at forty miles an hour while he sat still. He was moving through time and the only way to stop was to increase his velocity to match the speed of light. No one had offered him such a solution to his problems, which was proof he was on his own. In addition to the wind he felt, he could see other winds created by butterflies that moved through a meadow to his left. All objects on earth contributed to the gravity tugging at Loren. If those butterflies had flown through a different field, he'd have felt lighter. If they'd been hogs, he'd have felt heavier. These laws were indisputable, and he'd known them for some time; what he hadn't considered was that the higher he went, the farther from this valley, the lighter he'd be. Otherwise he'd sit on a porch at age seventy wanting to spell these thoughts across Chilhowee Mountain.

He got out of the truck at Papaw's house, the highest point on the whole property. Nowhere on Ruby's or Mother's or Cass's inheritance was higher. Someday soon a rich man would build a house on this hilltop; Papaw didn't seem to care. He stood near his chainsaw, looking at the peeling bark of a poplar, and Loren went on inside, letting the storm door slam behind him. He sat down in the bedroom and picked at the loose carpet, splitting strands in half and half again.

Papaw came in. Why'd you slam the door? he said.

I guess I just felt like it, said Loren.

Well, maybe I feel like it too.

Papaw grabbed the doorknob and slammed the door harder. Is that the way it was? he said, not really sounding upset. He was probably just bored. Loren didn't care. People came to him when they were bored. That was when they talked to him. It was true of Eli, Papaw, Ruby, Cass, Mr. Ownby, everyone. It was the only reason anyone cared about him. For that matter, it was the only reason anyone on earth cared about anyone else. It wasn't love, or affection, it was boredom. The same was true of every human relationship. The rest of humanity could behave as they wished, but he for one wasn't going to give people what they wanted. He stared at the blinds until eventually Papaw disappeared, and he was alone. He started beating his fists on the wall. As far as he could recall, it was the first time he'd beat his fists on anything. Experiences were good. Once upon a time, Mother had written them all down in his baby book, which would be bulldozed with the rest of his home. Eli was smart to want to drive a bulldozer. Loren would have Eli teach him someday when he was bored. Once he felt qualified to annihilate things, he'd steal a bulldozer at night and destroy whatever he wanted. But Eli didn't know how to operate bulldozers; it had been nothing but a desire. Loren would learn how to do it alone while Eli lay inside playing Nintendo. He supposed Eli was feeling extremely bored. There was no one to explain things to when Loren wasn't around. That was true for everyone in the family. They were fighting over who got to have him. He'd sell himself in a bidding war; then he'd run off anyway. That would show people.

He stayed in the room awhile, and then he went out to the front porch to compose his letter of departure. *To whom it may concern,* he wrote, *I don't know if you can even read this, but I'm not telling you where I'm going. I'm not telling you which way I'm heading. I'm not telling you what I'm taking with me. I'm not telling you whether I'll ever see you again.*

The note was only so they'd know not to look for him. Also he wanted his hardship to seem like a mystery to them. He was beginning to think they had more hardship than he anyway, but in that case, they needed to admit it to themselves. A cat howled from inside a stand of bushes in the yard, and Loren launched Papaw's bottle of gin toward the sound. We don't have a damn cat, he said. Inside, the refrigerator was buzzing louder to fill the empty space left by the cat. The storm door blew into the frame. Heat moved up the valley like a tidal wave. He heard a crash over by the old barn at the edge of the woods. Papaw's coke-bottle glasses lay on the front porch stoop. Loren tried them on, immediately staggering at their blurriness, then folded them into his pant pocket.

Hello? he called toward the barn.

He walked across the hilltop to it. For as long as Loren had been alive it had stood derelict. At some point all Papaw's land had been a farm. No one called it that anymore. None of the land remained cleared except for an acre of grass around the house so Mamaw could have her flowers. White irises were blooming now in clusters all over the yard. She had planted nothing but irises, because they were the state flower of Tennessee. She'd wanted all her flowers to look the same, which meant having just one kind, and she'd figured that might as well be the state flower. She probably wanted some transplanted to her grave. Too bad, thought Loren. He was done caring about dead people. He could think whatever thoughts he wanted without consequence. He could wish for people to die. It could be individual people or the entire population of a valley. It didn't have to be people at all; it could be Mamaw's irises. Now that she wasn't alive to separate their bulbs every few years, they'd stop blooming; anyway their outlook didn't look good, what with Dusty. For all intents and purposes, they were dead, as the farm had been for longer than Loren could know. He imagined animals in the barn, Papaw spreading sawdust on the carcasses of those animals. Cedar trees were growing in these woods, and cedars always thrived in soil drained of its nutrients. That supported the idea that the land had once been farmed, but Loren found it hard to imagine as he walked toward the sound he'd heard. Any paint that had ever covered the barn had worn away. Any cows milked here had died. A twenty-foot ladder was lying on the ground by the barn door. Hello, Loren said, hello. Hello. The ladder was too awkward to lift at first, but after a struggle, he managed to lean it against the barn's tin gutter. This would be the first time in his life he'd climbed a ladder. He reached the seventh rung before a head peeked over the roof. They stared at each other for a full minute before Loren said, What are you doing up there, and edged farther up the ladder.

Papaw made his way to the upper gambrel slope, blind without glasses, balancing with his arms, straddling the ridge like a fencepost rooster. Loren lifted himself over the cornice and wondered if Papaw hated the woods he faced, after so many years of staring at the same trunks. Barefoot, he navigated the rough, hot shingles.

You'll fall and break your neck, Loren said.

You don't fall and break your neck, said Papaw. You break your neck and then you fall.

Loren walked towards the obtuse joint of eaves where Papaw sat kicking his heels against the gable, bracing his face as if every rustle of tree limbs was a new, unnamed pain. He pressed his palm into a shingle as if to goad himself off the edge to the mud below.

You'll break your legs, said Loren.

They're done broke.

Loren sneaked up behind and placed the glasses onto Papaw's nose. He was glad they hadn't broken in his pocket. It nearly knocked Papaw sideways.

O Jesus, Papaw said when he saw how high he was. Get me down. O Lord.

He scooted back until he couldn't see over the edge. When a crow landed beside him, he cried out, scaring it off. His cheeks were drained of their former blood. He ran a hand across his head and said, I can't get down again.

Take the glasses back off, said Loren.

Papaw looked at Loren and sized him up from head to foot. I need a cigarette, he said.

They're down the ladder. I'll go down first and hold it steady.

Don't you touch me, Papaw said.

I'm trying to help you.

I'll kick you off.

Do it, then.

I'm sorry.

It's okay.

I can't go down.

Yes you can.

I could do it with a cigarette.

They're down at the house.

This is awful good of you, Loren.

When Papaw held the glasses in front of his eyes, they fogged up from his breath. Loren stepped back and looked down at the broken shingles of the roof. He wondered if the structure was strong enough to keep holding him up. Papaw wiped spit off his mouth with two fingers and coughed uncomfortably. As old as he was, he kept his jaw clenched up like he was twice that age, and Loren looked for signs of himself. It surprised him to see Venus in the sky beside Papaw's trembling face, a dot beneath the white sun. Few things took him by surprise anymore.

I think you're my best friend, said Papaw.

But you don't even like me.

He imagined touching Papaw's cheek to cultivate a tear, but it didn't seem like something that would happen. You've got real friends, he said.

Where? said Papaw.

Loren didn't know. He and Papaw looked out at the woods together.

Everyone else, said Papaw, all it is is secrets.

Fuck them and their secrets.

Papaw looked at him sidelong. You're seemin more like your mama these days, he said. Figger any kid of Avery's was venchly gonna turn out some way.

Loren descended to the house and found Papaw's cigarettes in a coat pocket. He could smell the flesh of all the trees mingling together. He thought of Ruby's prophecy that Papaw would die in three weeks. It had been about thirty-six hours. What was it he'd decided earlier; did Papaw pay attention to mysteries? He wasn't sure. He had ideas about what happened on the other side of the mountain: did that qualify as curiosity? He was worried and curious about Papaw at the same time. He could keep Papaw from jumping, or he could stand here and watch him jump. If he'd thought a jump likely, he might have chosen the latter option, but he decided to save Papaw instead. He climbed the ladder, stood on the roof, balanced himself with his arms, walked across the slope to Papaw, put a cigarette in Papaw's mouth, and lit it. There was a loud grinding noise in the distance that he assumed was bulldozers, and he sat beside his grandfather and watched for birds falling with the trees' white blossoms to be crushed.

Am I going to forget as much as you when I get old?

Probly, if you're lucky that is.

If Mother hadn't run off, would you ever have spent this much time with me?

She said you didn't want to see me none.

I guess I didn't.

That's when you was little, though. I guess it's been some changes since then.

I guess so, said Loren.

Back to forgettin, I reckon you could just die before you forget anything.

Loren decided to remember the woods. He counted the trees so he'd know in the future where they were rotting, fertilizing septic fields. He'd be aware that Mamaw's irises were blooming underground. New kids would move to Riverlake and join his class at school; someone else would be fat instead of Loren, and he'd be ready for it. His eyes were turning green. Mother's had done the same at his age, and maybe by now they'd changed to hazel or black. Why stop at only one part of the body; why not change all parts equally? She could have her ears replaced by man ears, her toes exchanged with someone else's, her blood traded for pig's blood. She ought to do it right. Papaw would understand that. Don't half-ass it, Loren thought. Carve off your whole skin and grow a new skin. Crust up and die. Just don't tell me about it, because I wouldn't understand.

If Mother disappeared forever, he asked, would you miss her?

I've done spent more time with you in a day as I have with her in four years.

But you knew where she lived. You could have come to visit.

I think as long as you know someone's there, you don't miss them.

I miss plenty of things that ain't there.

Does that mean you're sad about Mamaw?

Papaw shrugged. I reckon Mamaw's had her day in the sun.

Ruby thinks you'll die soon. She told me not to tell you. She thinks since Mamaw's dead, you'll die too within three weeks.

Loren didn't like being a tattletale, but he didn't think Ruby ought to sit around speculating on when people would pass, and he didn't want Papaw to die. Sitting on the barn roof with Papaw was the best thing that had happened to him in a long time. On the long walks to come, he'd remember how the sun felt good on him, how he lay on shingles running a finger around the loose waistline of his jeans, the smell of Papaw's cigarette smoke wafting above him on its way into nothing, as everything for miles around rested on the verge of destruction.

Ruby's tried to kill me plenty times before. Ain't nothing new.

She said you'd pine away and die. Not that she'd kill you.

I'm sure she prays for that every night before bedtime. It would make killing me awful easy on Ruby, if I was to pine away and die.

Loren was feeling brave in his questions. Do you care about your children? I mean, are you glad you had children?

They ain't been children for some years. I wasn't the one had children, it was Birdie. I reckon she'd be alive now if it weren't for all those children.

Did she really have twins, and one died?

Did your mama tell you that, or Ruby?

It was Mother who told me.

That Avery, I swear to the Lord, always did have a memory.

Loren pictured the faces of Papaw's three children side by side: Cass, Ruby, Avery. It was ludicrous to imagine a photograph of them together. As far as Loren knew, there was none of Mother, period. She liked it that way. Loren had wanted a camera for some time. You wouldn't know how to use one. You'd waste my money taking pictures of flowers. Cameras are too expensive. I don't like cameras. Stop trying to make me feel bad about my appearance.

He'd thought he could save the money himself by picking blackberries in summer and selling them door to door. In the meadows around his house grew bountiful harvests of blackberries; houses, though, were far between. Mother refused to drive him. I'd spend more on gas than you'd make on berries. When it came down to it, Loren hadn't wanted to sweat through weeds in the heat getting cut by thorns. His memory would remain strong enough to take the place of a camera. I'm glad you gave it up about that camera. If there's one thing I never did like, it's cameras. As if there wasn't enough on earth to waste a dollar on, here comes cameras.

The blackberries that year were spent on starlings that spread the seeds across the fields and into Loren's backyard, which was soon covered in stalks of thorns. The berries on those stalks existed currently as flowers and were in for a big surprise. Loren couldn't remember why he'd begun to remember this. Something about family. The idea of photographs. He laughed out loud thinking of a family photograph. It made sense that there wasn't one. He hadn't meant to end his aloneness by considering it, but things had been ending for quite some time. They weren't going to quit anytime soon. Vultures were flying lazy eights around the sun, looking for someone to eat, and it wasn't long before they seemed to have found someone. Loren looked over the edge of the roof and saw Eli, Cass, and Ruby squinting up at him, heading toward the ladder. Of course. They were here to reclaim him. The fight could begin. In the heat of it, he'd sneak away. Ruby was carrying a black leather briefcase. She trampled irises as she walked, because she wouldn't look at the ground, but Eli did it on purpose. Ruby tucked the briefcase under her arm and began to climb the ladder. Loren was glad to see how long it took her to climb. Someday he'd be better than everyone. When she reached the top, she seemed pleased somehow that Papaw was on the roof; she shook her head and said, Daddy. I swear.

You swear? You're too chickenshit to swear.

Then how about, Daddy, I fucking swear.

Avery's the one who could swear. You can't swear worth a damn.

I don't give a shit how you think I swear.

I don't give a shit whether you give a shit.

She opened the briefcase as Cass pulled himself onto the roof. She had brought some papers for Papaw to sign. It was a big stack, with about thirty different places to sign.

So they're gonna let me put my songs on the mountain, Papaw said.

Is that what it says there on that page?

If I'm askin a question, I intend you should answer.

Daddy, I'd always suspected you couldn't read, and now I know.

I can read everything, clear as day, Papaw said, as Eli scrambled onto the roof. I made everything the way it was, long before you popped out.

Here, Daddy, pretend you're a helpless little crippled retarded child and I'm telling you what to do. Here's the pen. Take the pen. Hold out your hand.

You gonna let her talk to you that way? said Cass, who still stood by the edge, facing away from it. He didn't seem to realize how close he was to falling.

Cass, said Papaw, I could push you off of this barn. He turned to Ruby. It's like a baby in a candy shop, he said. You don't wanna give it no candy, but it bawls and bawls and finally you just give it the damn candy to shut it up.

So sign it, Daddy. Give me the candy.

Avery's signed it too? Or did you forge it like you do everything else?

Ruby glanced at Loren. I have something for you, she told
him.

Don't listen to her, said Eli, it's a trick.

Ruby handed Loren an envelope that had been cut open.

You've got the stupidest family in the world, Eli told Loren.
What are they all doing up top of a barn? What is all this?

I was doing fine up here by myself.

It's us against them.

What is it you want me to do?

Push everybody off the roof. I'll help. You've got to start,
though.

Loren watched how Eli's chin stood up, how he breathed so
slowly, eight or fewer breaths a minute. Eli cared as much about
Loren as Loren did about him. It was the first time that had happened with anyone Loren's own age; anyone who had a body,
anyway. Maybe he and Eli were about to become blood broth-
ers. It didn't matter, though. He wasn't planning to take Eli with
him when he ran away.

Go on, Lorn, open the envelope.

The clouds were evaporating into a blinding intensity, so
everyone had to shut their eyes. Eli's jaw caught the sunlight
and shadowed his neck. Time moved quickly only for bad
things, and Loren tried to slow his intake of air to match the
slowness of everything around him. Fine, said Ruby, I don't care
about you either, and she put the pen in Papaw's limp hand and
helped him sign the papers one by one. Loren could read a few
of their words at the edge of his vision. He saw that someone
had signed with the name Avery Garland. There it was again on
the next page: Avery Garland. In order to have a mystery, he
thought, you had to care about the people whose lives were being solved. He moved to the other end of the roof. His pants

were falling down. He tightened his belt a notch and sat facing west. The bickering behind him evolved with the passing of time and took on greater complexity. He lay down so that the skyline sank a millimeter. With his finger he collected dirt into a snake and slid it link by link to the roof's edge. Snakes disintegrated into wind when they fell off cliffs, their teeth and scales the same disembodied dust. I don't know what that's supposed to mean, Ruby was yelling, and Loren put two fingers to his forehead as he watched the sun and lost her words in thinner and thinner clouds until suddenly Cass was slapping his arm as if only to prove he was still around.

Why's your hand on your head like that?

Loren pointed out at the mountain.

The mountain hurts your head? said Cass.

When Loren gestured to the dimming land, he realized he could never explain what he'd meant. He stared at a point two thumblengths from the sun so that light danced formlessly on his eyelids. His legs were numb; he wondered if his blood would stop circulating. The shape of Ruby's hair had collapsed from the heat. You'll get your Duraliner bed for your truck, she was saying. Loren used his finger to work a booger down his septum, then flicked it away for the crows to eat. He watched his family's necks sway gently as the trees behind them blurred across the landscape. He hadn't wanted to cry all week. He looked at the letter some more. Eli came over and curled his arm around Loren, because he was Eli's only ally here, he supposed. Rather than looking into Eli's eyes, he stared between them, so Eli would feel the way Loren himself had felt for his whole life.

Loren? Have you ever wished for a twin brother?

They observed each other as if each could see the other's thoughts. Really Loren saw only the distant rise of Parsons Bald. He'd always imagined that I was his twin. After all, Mother had created us both. There was a time when we'd looked kind of like each other. He had wanted to be a girl, and I'd just wanted to have a body, any body, so our desires at least were twinned to each other. In some languages, *snake* and *twin* were the same word. But there was no way Eli could have known about me. Loren looked down at the grass, really looked at it. It moved only when he moved. He saw how much everything had changed. At one time Eli would have said he didn't see how Mother could feed both of them at once. Would his twin be fat too? Everyone would like the thin twin better, even Mother. But he didn't say it, and it wasn't true, as I think I've proven. Loren wouldn't hate knowing what his thin face would look like, and he wouldn't be jealous, and I wouldn't be able to make fun of him better than anyone just because I knew him so well, and Mother wouldn't like me more than him. None of that would be true.

No, Loren said. I don't think so.

I have, said Eli.

Loren didn't know what to say.

It's stupid to worry about it, though, said Eli. There's nothing that can change.

So many thoughts, all the time. Loren wondered how stupid people even dealt with it, how they remembered to breathe in and out. He stood and spread his arms in the sun and walked to the edge. He wanted mountains all around him, not on just one side. He tried to think about something calm, but there was nothing, so he changed his mind. An airplane's red light blinked across the sky. He thought he heard machines in the woods, but Papaw said it was just nuclear waste from the bomb tests. It had deformed people for miles around. They'd grown eyes like dartboards, seven skeletons, big white assholes that glowed in the dark. Loren watched for metal pincers to reach down from the sky to clamp his life out. He could feel the future deaths of the trees. He could feel the deaths of future squirrels. If the county lost its trees the sky would seem bigger, but really the hills would just be smaller. Papaw's face cast shadows like the last remaining pillar of a forest. Loren looked at the envelope some more. It bore his name in cursive script, which he read forwards and backwards. He read it so many times he lost count. Backwards it was neroL. Upside down it was illegible. He stared until he had read it infinitely. He began to have a deep understanding of his own name: he wasn't defined by it, it was meaningless, the person who'd given it to him didn't know its meaning. He pulled a sheet of spiral notebook paper from the envelope. Both sides had script in pencil lead. Where were you when I dammed the mountain creeks, he read.

Why does this start on page twenty? he asked.

Ruby looked at him, startled. Maybe Avery can't count, she said.

There's just two pages, though.

There's a two in twenty, said Ruby.

Probly she went and told the truth about us all, said Papaw.

So where is it? demanded Loren. Where'd you put it?

What, said Papaw, the truth? I'd say Ruby burned it all up.

I want it back. I'm tired of this.

Lorn, said Ruby, you know all the truth about me that you will ever know.

Loren could see the whole valley from where he sat. He saw Dusty's contractor pushing a chainwheel through Papaw's front yard. He saw fruit trees, dogwoods, swollen pines. He saw the mountain and the knobs. The sun was beginning to set in the distance above Tellico Lake. Papaw sucked his cigarette straight to the filter and sent it searing toward the trees. He sang his old maids song again. They sat on a cot. They sat on a patch. They sat in a pit. He lit another cigarette. He talked the whole time he smoked it, but Loren didn't listen anymore, because he realized now that Papaw was using the same few words over and over.

so now maybe you'll understand if I say why I acted the way I did. Like back when you were little. I told you you had three eyes and I said the third one was always closed. You looked in the glass and I said, it's closed now. You turned away and I said, now it's open again. You looked in the glass and I said, now it's closed again. But I started to feel bad about it. It was the same thing Daddy did to me and I thought well I'd better raise you the same way. I thought if I raised you the same way, you'd be tough like me. I told Daddy Cass and Ruby don't ever tell the truth about his eye. When Daddy used to do it to me I could never see the eye. All I had was a forehead. So that's what I did to you. But you got all sensitive about it like I was supposed to be your best friend. Like we were the same age as each other. I was just trying to help. I knew you wouldn't remember anything from that early in your life, but you couldn't deal with someone being in control. So I'm supposed to be nice to you. Well I know about the world and I had reasons for being that way. I had a plan for you. If you'd just wait till you were old enough to remember. Maybe in a few more years. But you were a coward about it, so I gave up and started being nice. I'm trying to tell you that's the opposite. Then you started talking to Luther. I got scared you wouldn't even want me around anymore. I know what I am and what people think of me. I know what every single person in this world thinks of me. I couldn't handle it for you to think that way too. I just couldn't bear the thought of it. I figured if I just shut my eyes and didn't tell you anything, it would turn out. You had each other. You and Luther. So I thought I'd see if you really needed someone like me. You think that's suffering? Where were you when I was growing up? Where were you when I dealt with all these people? You think you were around for my whole life? You think the fact you care for me makes up for all the time I was alone? Of course you care about me. That's the way it is. You think that makes you special? I'm just trying to tell you something about what my life is. Why can't

I teach you to be strong without you crying about it? How can I teach you anything if I've got to announce I'm only doing it to teach you? You really think we'd be friends if you'd been born when I was born, if you're this way all the time? Look who I had around back then. They acted like they weren't even real. I didn't belong here. I wanted to find who died the day that I was born and why he climbed inside the wrong body to live somewhere else while I'm here sweating. But I still wanted you to like this place for some reason. So that I wouldn't sign the papers. You don't know a hickory from an oak. I hate to know the names of things. I have these dreams where the names of everything are written as words on whatever it's a name of. You're not the only one who has nightmares you know. I have this one dream where you and Luther are falling off of Look Rock Tower. You're falling at the same rate. That's how I know you're the same as each other. You hold hands while you fall. I wake up sweating. I've spent my life trying to do things. When I was little I dammed the creeks so everyone would drown, but they didn't drown. No one made enough sense to drown. They'd have just floated. I figure you think the same about me. When I was little, Daddy told me I had a dead twin. You smothered it up inside of your mama, he said. He always told Ruby the same thing. Sometimes he told it to Cass. So I told you the same too and I don't feel bad about it. That's what I did and it's the past. You believed anything. You missed your dead twin. In Africa they take their baby twins into the woods and leave them for the birds to eat. Why do you think I'm on the earth at all? It's too late for me. I'm already the way I am. Whatever I do, it won't really change. I thought maybe you'd grow up and find a cure for being trapped inside yourself. So I told you about this twin and how he'd struggled as he drowned. I just wanted to put something into the world for you. You started talking to it more than you talked to me. You told it the words I'd said. You only liked me because you had to, but you liked Luther for no reason at all. When *he was mean to you, you liked him. When I was mean to you, you cried. You only liked me when I gave you whatever you wanted. If I told you what was really going on, I thought, you wouldn't like me. No one else has ever understood it, so there's no reason you would, either. I just let you have what you wanted and gave up. You had these awful dreams about me. You told me about it like I was supposed to feel bad for you. There was one where I fell off the mountain and hit the bottom and exploded. Pieces of me went everywhere and stuck to the rocks. You woke up and started crying. Promise me you won't jump off the mountain, you said. Just promise. Swear on your life. Stop being silent. They can't bury you if you're in little pieces. Well I never thought of jumping till you told me to. I'd thought of other things, but not that. That was something you put in my mind all by yourself. I started to think on that same path. I wondered if that was what you wanted for me. That's my punishment for creating the world for you. Or for not creating it sooner. You think I hide my past from you. Where were you when I dammed the mountain creeks? Maybe I needed you then. Where were you when the mimosas grew faster than I did? Chilhowee Mountain would have been our pasture. We'd have watched hawks circling through the valley for prey. Dropping blood on what they had slain. We'd have run away from these people. They've been looking at me their whole lives. I can feel my third eye, between my real eyes, where they look at me. Remember when we bought your funeral suit at Proffitt's, you stared at those older boys from town. I didn't want you to think they'd like you, or it would break my heart when you found out they never would. You watched their shoulder blades swaying as they strolled away. I wanted you to get it in mind early. I've already been around. I know how it is. I made you in my image. We walked back to the car and they didn't notice you staring. I don't think you understand how it makes me feel to know how it is for you. To watch people laugh at you. I wanted to kill whoever laughed. When we got home, I baked a cake to make you feel better. You ate about three pieces of it. Then you started whispering to Luther again. I wished I could tell you the truth. I tried to think of just one thing to say that wouldn't embarrass me. But I didn't lie to you, either. I left things out, but I haven't lied in years. Maybe I'll lie to you now, so that when I get home, I'll have a good, sound reason to tell the truth.*

There's a lake here at Top of the World where I can walk along the shore and look at the vista. I can see radio towers blinking red and in the distance I see Maryville. I don't like it here, though. This is the kind of mountain where no one ever built wings to try to soar to the horizon like a falcon. Not even thousands of years ago, before airplanes, when it would have been worth trying. When they dig our land up, look for buried wings among the bones. There won't be any, because no one has tried it. No one felt that they needed to. That's just the kind of place this mountain is. But I guess you can tell I'm not on any mountain. You're pretty smart, and I bet you can figure that out. On that mountain, people are either smart or they're strong. One or the other. I guess I was hoping you'd learn to be both.

Loren saw that Mother had caused none of his suffering, because his suffering was what he'd been through here for the past two weeks. She had nothing to do with it except that she'd created him. That was something that should never have been doubted.

But inside himself, a slow buzzing of a voice was putting him through some inner violence that made him doubt all of his exciting new thoughts, and that voice was mine. I thought if I could make him feel me when he slipped into what his body wanted him to be, he'd move away from his body and into his mind again, where I am. Loren had never liked violence, though, especially if it lived inside him. And his relief at the evidence of Mother's continued existence was so great that he had a hard time imagining me anymore. There was no need to imagine anything when what mattered to him was already real. The greatest revelation of the letter was the one he ignored: that Mother had been trying to do the same thing to him that I was doing. I couldn't believe it. I hadn't thought she was strong enough to accept what comes from confronting the world that way, but she'd accepted it. It was just that she was incapable of achieving her goal. Only in leaving had she succeeded. Now that she was coming back, I saw a future in which everything would crumble. Loren would live with her again. He didn't know yet that this would happen. They'd be happier together, now that he was learning the truth about her. She'd feed him twice as much as before. Someone else would live there too. They'd be one big happy family. He'd never go hungry. He imagined the abundance. Whatever was necessary to spend time with her, that was what would happen.

What do you need from the store, Loren?

Maybe some peanut butter. You forgot it last time, you know.

I imagined him digging into it with a spoon, excavating as much as he could fit on the spoon. He licks the spoon, looking at her as he licks it. She asks for one too. He digs her a spoon. Together they lick their spoons. The peanut butter tastes much better now that he's had a taste of what it is to be hungry. With the remaining profits from the land, Mother promises she'll fill the pantry for the rest of his childhood. They smile at each other, and this is the rule of law. Loren will never be mine.

I guess the whole thing was predetermined all along, but that doesn't mean I'm not disappointed. It had never occurred to me that our Mother might tell the truth. Once you tell the truth, and the truth is the truth that it is, and people are still with you, then that's the end, and I give up; there's nothing left for me in this valley. In fact I'm disgusted with the whole world; I leave it to the tyrants, so that they might experience the one thing I ever wanted. Not that I feel sorry for myself. I could keep seeking that thing in another place, but I've been watching people find it for my entire existence, and I'm tired of the jealousy. I've had enough of it. I feel sated. Maybe that's not as nice as having a companion, but I did lose, and a sense of satiety, if one is forced to continue to live, is better, I suppose, than feeling nothing at all.

Acknowledgments

I would like to thank the following people and organizations for their wisdom and inspiration and support and encouragement: Madison Smartt Bell, Elizabeth Spires, Pinckney Benedict, Jeanne Larsen, Richard Dillard, David Bradley, Aiden Faust, Jaina Hirai, Dan Stern, Lesley Wernsdorfer, Jenny Noller, J. T. Hill, Kathleen Johnson, the Mrs. Giles Whiting Foundation, Jeff Severs, Haven Iverson, Sue Batterton, Emily Rapp, Liz Phang, Sara Smith, Peter Short, Steve Slattery, Brendan Short, Michael Dickman, Steve Moore, Carrie Fountain, Kirk Lynn, Khaled Mattawa, Lisa Railsback, Paola Fantini, Dan Basila, Jason Spence, Jim Magnuson, Michael Adams, Steve Harrigan, Joy Williams, Denis Johnson, the James A. Michener Center for Writers, Naomi Shihab Nye, Josh Kendall, and Jane Gelfman.